SLIPPING

MOHAMED KHEIR

TRANSLATED BY
ROBIN MOGER

SLIPPING

TWO LINES
PRESS

Originally published as إفلات الأصابع
© 2019 by al Kotob Khan Publishing & Distribution
Translation copyright © 2021 by Robin Moger

Two Lines Press
582 Market Street, Suite 700, San Francisco, CA 94104
www.twolinespress.com

Cover design by Gabriele Wilson
Cover: detail of the painting *I Love the Life* by Hossam Dirar.
© Hossam Dirar, used by permission of the artist
Design by Sloane | Samuel
Printed in Canada

ISBN: 978-1-949641-16-5
Ebook ISBN: 978-1-949641-17-2

Library of Congress Cataloging-in-Publication Data

Names: Kheir, Mohamed, 1978– author. | Moger, Robin, translator.
Title: Slipping / Mohamed Kheir; translated by Robin Moger.
Other titles: Iflāt al-asābiʻ. English
Identifiers: LCCN 2020037894 (print) | LCCN 2020037895 (ebook)
ISBN 9781949641165 (trade paperback) | ISBN 9781949641172 (ebook)
Subjects: LCSH: Egypt--Social conditions--Fiction.
GSAFD: Suspense fiction.
Classification: LCC PJ7942.H42 I3513 2021 (print)
LCC PJ7942.H42 (ebook) | DDC 892.7/37--dc23
LC record available at https://lccn.loc.gov/2020037894
LC ebook record available at https://lccn.loc.gov/2020037895

1 3 5 7 9 10 8 6 4 2

PART ONE

WE WALKED ON WATER AND MET A STRANGER

1

HIS COMMANDS

From behind the glass the cold meat called to him, seemed to him in that moment—in the heat, midway through his fast—like a dollop of red Chantilly cream, set to melt in the mouth as soon as it was laid there. He thought he might cook it in the narrow alley outside his building, then tried to remember where he'd put the grill, and couldn't. But when he got home there was a surprise: his mother, bustling about the kitchen between cutting boards and cooking pots. The first time she'd been in the kitchen since his father's death.

She saw the bag of beef hanging from his hand. "Put it in the fridge," she said wearily. "Your father said to cook duck."

For one shaken instant Ahmed doubted his sanity. "He came to me in a dream," his mother said simply. "He was sitting in the big chair in front of the television, wearing his Eid robe, and he tells me, 'Let's have a couple of ducks, Sayyida.' I said, 'Duck's too rich

when you've been fasting. It'll give you indigestion.'
But he insisted: 'I want ducks. They're in season.'

"So I said, 'Fine.'"

And his father had turned back to the television
while she wept herself awake.

Then she'd gotten up, taken herself to the nearest
town, collected the pensions (her pension and his),
and, on the way back to the village, stopped by the
window in the wall of the government store where
she purchased the ducks and the ingredients she
needed to cook them. Back home, she'd flipped the
light switch in the kitchen and just stood there, knees
trembling, in the doorway.

A whole life spent here, and now it felt as though
she were a stranger to it; a newcomer.

Within minutes, though, the illusion of unfamil-
iarity had melted away, ceding its place to sweet and
sweaty absorption in the cramped kitchen's heat.

They broke their fast by wolfing part of the first duck,
putting the rest in the fridge for later. The other duck
she gave to a neighbor.

"He told you to do that, too?" Ahmed asked.

"No, no," she said. "Raqiya's been my rock. I prom-
ised myself she'd eat from the first meal I cooked."

He nodded and went to his room to get some
sleep before the night shift started.

Two days later he looked in on her to ask if he could
get her anything, and she said, "What's that shirt,
Ahmed? Wear the blue one."

She'd dreamed about him the night before. Him and his father. They had been laughing together and his father had taken something from his pocket and handed it to Ahmed, who'd peered down at the thing, a look of delight on his face. He had been wearing the blue shirt.

"Wear the blue, my boy," she repeated, "God will bless your day."

And so it was—starting the day of the ducks, some four months since his passing—that Ahmed's father reestablished himself in the house: dictating what they ate, prodding them to visit this relative or that, sharing the location of old documents that lay hidden in drifts of loose paper and junk. And as time went on, these edicts started to touch on more serious matters. For instance, the demand—couched in the same coded language of dreams—that his son give up his night job. Ahmed was distraught at first, then settled into bitter resentment. His stomach problem, a constant companion while his father was still alive, came back. He kept expecting to see him sitting in the living room, or run into him on the way to the bathroom, and whenever he hung back from fulfilling these dream-conveyed commands, his mother would wail, "God protect you, my boy!" in a tone of genuine apprehension. And in those words, an insinuation: divine protection was entirely dependent on the father not being provoked, even in death.

The suspicion that she might be fabricating these dreams crept into his thoughts, then crystallized.

Specifically, the time she interpreted a dream to mean he should stay away from a girl he was thinking of marrying, followed by another girl, soon after. *Father wouldn't care who I married*, he told himself, his doubts growing. And though he lacked the courage to confront her, he had begun to think of her revelations as lies. At times, the waves of suspicion would swell and he'd be angry at her; at others, they'd settle, and the anger would turn on his father, lording over their household from the grave.

Just as he was considering leaving home altogether, his father came to him in a dream. It was the first time he had come to Ahmed: He stood mournfully at Ahmed's bedroom door and nodded toward the room where he himself had once slept.

"Get up," he said. "Wake your mother."

2

THE PASSERS-BY DON'T CARE WHAT WE DO

Clouds inched across the sky as though afraid they'd spill, while down below I strained to keep up with Bahr's short-legged but rapid clip.

In Muharram Bey, he led me down a narrow street with wide balconies beneath its windows before coming to a halt outside a huge, silent building which ran the length of a block, and there we lingered for a moment. Bahr appeared to be thinking. Then off he set again, trotting along until we came to a broad avenue aglow in the pale sunlight of early winter.

Alexandria's aging buildings sagged into one another, yellowed and peeling. They were set back from the road on either side, and between them lay a great network of streetcar lines, crossing and recrossing like a tracery of veins. Bahr picked a path through the tracks, and cautiously I followed. I followed him over rail after rail, while he kept his gaze fixed on the ground as though trying to marry a memory to what he saw.

Suddenly, he stopped, whispered, "Here!" and tugged at me so that I was standing bolt upright, directly behind him. Then I heard it, the distant but distinctive metallic tick of streetcar wheels approaching, and as that grew louder, an identical ticking, echoing the first, started to close in from somewhere behind us.

From where I stood, looking out over the top of Bahr's head, I could see one streetcar coming from our right, and another, its twin, running in from the left. Both were making straight for us, and my knees began to tremble involuntarily.

"Bahr?"

For a few seconds he said nothing, then:

"Shut your eyes if you want."

But I couldn't bring myself to shut my eyes, and once again I steeled myself to face the gathering madness of the mission ahead. The ticking grew louder and the ground trembled, flecks of gravel hopped and flew, and the approaching cars began to pick up speed. I wanted to run, but it was too late. I might lose my way amid the forest of tracks; might end up on the wrong line. I stayed put.

First to reach us was the streetcar to the right. Its ancient, dilapidated snout kinked our way ever so slightly, a deviation that brought it almost close enough to brush us as it passed, and I saw—or thought I saw—the driver on his raised stool, gazing down at us with absolute impassivity. And then the second arrived, rolling down rails that seemed only slightly set off from the tracks the first had taken, and it kinked too, a few millimeters away from us this time, and went on by, car after car looming over us, yellow as the shadows of the buildings lining the road. If we'd shifted even a centimeter we would have been run down.

We stood in a roughly circular and impossibly tiny clearing bracketed by the cars. The racket from the wheels was tremendous, Death was breathing very close, and the daylight vanished behind the roof of each passing carriage, then reappeared. And in the flickering light, I saw her: sitting at her sewing machine in a nightgown, squinting at me.

She said, "You've grown, Seif." She sounded surprised.

Then she disappeared, a star winking out, and it felt as though the passing carriages would never come to an end. What if Bahr had miscalculated? What if the rails with their central jutting tooth were to shift, just a fraction? What if one—too old, perhaps, or poorly maintained—were to buckle or bend? Was this what suicides felt in the last seconds before impact? Did they see what I was seeing, or did shock claim them before the shock of steel?

And then, at last, the streetcars were gone. An "at last" that marked the end of no more than a few seconds, but even so I patted at my hair, perhaps to feel whether the patch of rougher gray had spread. But Bahr seemed invigorated. "The safe point," as he called it, pointing to a page in his notebook, still existed. Was it the product of pure chance, or had some engineer put it there on purpose, as some kind of secret game? And who had first discovered it?

Before I could ask, Bahr laid his hand on my shoulder and nodded toward the place where we'd been standing, where the two lines parted and rejoined. He gave me a wink and asked, "Did you see anything, Seif?" Still pale, I stayed silent, so he asked again, his smile widening:

"Who was it?"

My voice was a whisper, "My mother."

He stared at me blankly for a second, then nodded slowly. His expression seemed to reflect a trace of disappointment and he opened his mouth as though to speak before seeming to reconsider. At last, lips thin, he muttered, "Typical!"

Still stunned, I didn't reply. Just looked at him: the neat gray hair, the odd red glasses, the vigor I attributed to a life spent out of doors. Nothing at all like a man who would be gone within a month. Not that I knew that then, though I can't now summon the memory without the fact of his absence surfacing through it.

Between dream and waking is where I see us, forever standing beneath that soft sunlight in Muharram Bey, my tongue too heavy to warn him.

3

WHERE WERE YOU, ALI?

The first thing he knew was that a great black rock was resting its full weight on his chest and head, and for a moment he assumed, as was usually the case in his nightmares, that he had died. For the briefest fraction of a second he thought it must be the sleep paralysis, which held his body in its grip whenever he went to bed too tired, but when he tried to wiggle his finger the tip responded, and so did his elbow when he tried to flex it, then his whole arm moved, and then he summoned his courage and cracked open a lid. A dazzle of sunlight. A scatter of flies hanging mid-air. Turning his head, he saw that he was lying in the dirt surrounded by garbage. A dump perhaps? He appeared to be lying in a shallow trench, scraped a few centimeters deep into the packed earth. Pain at the back of his head and in his joints. His chest was tight.

The ground beneath him began shaking and then there was a furious clanging as if of church bells, a sound which resolved itself into a train's bell, the next instant supplanted by the din of a horn blaring at a tremendous pitch and drawing closer and more powerful every second. Seized with terror, he shut his eyes but then opened them again to see a train's hulking mass rush by very close to his right, its horn battering his ears, and then, before his heartbeat could return to normal, the train was away into the distance, then gone. He pushed himself up from the ground and stood.

He looked around and saw no one. Some way off, the indistinct form of a bird dipped low to the ground then rose up and flapped away.

Where am I, and what now?

With a little effort he managed to remember his name, and checking himself all over he found no wounds, despite the pain. Another look around. Nothing but distant rooftops and the snaking tracks. Then, blossoming inside him without warning, a thought: *Noha! What's happened to her?*

Then he remembered. Remembered everything but the one thing he needed to remember.

He had just finished trimming his hair and shaving over at his friend's apartment. His family was at home, waiting for him, and Noha's family was at her place, also waiting for him. He was due to go over to her place with his family, pick her up from the hair salon on the ground floor of her apartment building, then head over to the wedding venue, thus bringing an end to a journey of patience and longing and exhaustion and—for her—of terror. *He wouldn't leave her, would he?* A thought she'd brooded over daily and which had made him laugh to hear, because his heart had been hers from the moment they met.

He'd left his friend and taken a shortcut home, where he put on the suit another friend had sold to him at a discount. Joy was nearly in his grasp; joy, or at any rate, relief.

Among the last things he remembered seeing: children running with metal hoops; a pickup being loaded from a small bar; a pair of young women walking together; another woman watering her plants on a balcony overhead and the water dripping to the ground.

He had gone around the back of the gray building on the corner of Awqaf Street, down a narrow lane without doors or windows, emerged on the far side, and turned right, starting to lengthen his stride. He had thought that he'd heard a woman's voice calling out, but turning to look had seen only darkness.

Where are you, Ali? What time is it? There was his watch on his right wrist, miraculously unstolen. It was when he looked at it that the terror found him. Twelve-thirty, and the hot sun overhead told him that it was half-past noon, not midnight.

You left your friend's apartment at five in the evening. A night's gone by, Ali. A whole night has passed and left you here, in day. The watch must be right: the sun, and you're famished. A whole night. Noha waiting for you, surrounded by her family. A whole night and you never came.

God!

He could feel his cellphone in his pocket and he took it out. It was off. When he tried switching it on, nothing happened—so thoroughly dead it might never have been charged at all—and inside he felt a new fear rise up that he quickly suppressed. He searched his pockets. Here was his wallet, his identity card. Everything where it should be, so what had happened? *What am I doing here?* He looked around. *Where is here, anyway?*

And where is everybody else? The question suggested itself because the buildings, which he had now reached, appeared to be completely empty, even of ghosts. Walking slowly, he saw not a single human being, young or old or in-between, and as he made his way between the buildings he started at the sound of doors clapping in the breeze. Building after building with nothing to hear, nothing to see.

Had the world come to an end?

But then he remembered the train.

Wandering along something resembling a highway, he spotted a sign lying on the ground and caked in dirt. He wiped the dust from the letters with his shoe and read the name of a place he'd never heard of. He kept walking. He sighed with relief when the first truck went by. But no one stopped for him and so on he went until, up ahead, he saw the outskirts of another town.

He felt better when he saw a child playing on the doorstep of a house, and then people began to appear, singly and in small groups, on foot and in vehicles. He still had no idea where he was. He became conscious of the fact that his clothes and face were covered with dirt, and he paused to brush it off.

There was a woman selling vegetables from a stall. He walked up to her, right up to the face behind its niqab, but then kept walking. He was afraid to tell anyone he was lost. They might take advantage of him. They might be suspicious.

He found a little coffee shop with a cart set up outside selling chopped liver, so he bought a couple of sandwiches and sat down. The man from the coffee shop brought him a glass of water, then a glass of tea, and the tiny television was on, so Ali shifted his chair closer to see what he could see, to try and understand what was going on, but the news reports told him nothing. Then he saw the date and realized that it was Sunday, and the legs that had carried him from his friend's place on Thursday evening began to shake.

He'd lost three days, not one. What was happening? What had happened to him? To the world? Noha?

Later, he would hear everything. He would hear about the faintings and nervous breakdowns, the fury that raged through her household, about the humiliations and insults endured by his family. He would be told about the hours spent waiting in the apartments and at the venue, about the departure, first of the maazoun, then of the guests. About the shock of friends, the fretting of relatives. He would learn that they had disappeared, Noha and her family, the family apartment shut up and abandoned. He would meet his mother's tears, his father's silence, the deluge of his siblings' questions and their demands for answers—some explanation for those three days gone. And it would seem to him then that the whole world had been reduced to just those four words: Where were you, Ali?

Not a cut or a bruise anywhere on his body. Nothing stolen. All the time he'd been gone, no stranger had come around demanding a ransom; there'd been no menacing calls. Something had happened to him. If it had killed him, it would at least have left his dignity intact. But nothing had happened to him. He'd emerged from an alley, heard a woman's voice, and then come to on a patch of packed earth somewhere between Cairo and Alexandria. Then he had gone home: materializing on the corner of his street like a djinn, like a premonition of disaster.

And they had returned, dizzy from their rounds of the hospitals and clinics and police stations and homes of friends and acquaintances, to find the missing man in perfect health: not a scratch on him, and nothing to soothe their anger.

4

WE WALKED ON WATER AND MET A STRANGER

Where the corniche wall ran out, a great tree hooped over to drink from the river. Beyond the tree there was nothing: nothing between us and the water.

We walked by the light of the stars, to our left a scattering of buildings, silent as though abandoned and none more than two stories high. There was the soft howling of dogs in the distance, and the rustle of small things, some living, from the ground. All of a sudden, Bahr halted and pulled me to one side, right to the lip of the riverbank. For a moment it was as if he wanted me to leap into the Nile, but then I saw a flight of stone steps in the starlight, appearing as if from nowhere: narrow, running from the embankment where we stood down to the water's surface, to where there was no jetty, no boat, no hut, nothing: as though inviting us under.

Without saying a word, Bahr cautiously began his descent and I followed. When he came to the second to last step, just before he reached the water, he sat down. I took the step above him, and we leaned back against the wall. Bahr said, "It was against a wall like this, on steps like these, that I kissed a girl for the first time."

I listened, waiting for him to go on, but he was done. In that silence it felt as though the stars were humming for us, lullabying, soothing us to sleep.

Out in the heart of the river's darkness there was a movement, and we sat up, suddenly alert. Then, to our astonishment—or at least, to mine—we saw him: a man coming across the river, walking on water. Bahr got to his feet. "Now," he said, placing his feet on the final step so the water lapped at his shoes. Then he stooped and slipped them off and, without turning around, told me, "Take off your shoes, Seif."

My quaking heart.

The man drew closer. He was wearing a robe with the hem held up over his knees and, like Bahr, seemed to be holding shoes or slippers in one hand. He stepped carefully, and I could see that with each step the water just covered the round of his heel.

When the man reached us he stopped. "Assalamu aleikom." We returned the greeting, and then, Bahr shrinking back to give him space, he carefully placed his foot on the bottom step. He examined us for a moment, and it was as though he were on the verge of asking us something, but he seemed to reconsider, and climbed past us to the top of the riverbank—the height of a roof above us—and wandered away.

Now Bahr extended a foot and placed it on the

face of the river, into which it sunk until the water rose over the heel, exactly as it had on the feet of the man in the robe. He set the second foot beside the first, took a step, and nodded. Smiled.

"Let's go."

My bare sole descended a few centimeters through river water and came to rest on a slippery surface. Later, I would learn, that for a period just before dawn when the dam's floodgates upriver were closed, the water level would drop and the river thin. At some point, the locals had worked out that for those few minutes a raised stretch of riverbed was brought right to the surface and, in that brief interval before the floodgates reopened and the raised bed sank back beneath the rising water, they could use it as a shortcut. They'd walk from dry land to dry land seeming, to those not from this place, like prophets or saints: striding splendidly yet humbly over the waves.

As I dipped my foot to follow Bahr I knew none of this.

I went carefully, watching the Nile's gentle waves in the moon's light and trying to make out the sound they made, trying to remember the particular word for that sound. Was it *ajeej*? *Haad*? What had Alya called it? I tried to picture her saying the word and then imitating the sound. Singing it.

This was long before Bahr. I had awoken after a night spent in a friend's apartment, to find that my friend wasn't there. Not to say that I felt any of the fleeting trauma of opening your eyes somewhere unfamiliar—no: it was with a sense of belonging that I got up and moved through the apartment in search of the bathroom. Which is when it reached me—the sweet strong sound of singing from somewhere beyond the living room.

A woman's voice, soft but with breadth, like an old-time dive-bar diva. And faint, too, like a murmur or a shifting of wings. Half-awake and half-bewitched, I followed the line of the song, and when I came to the kitchen doorway I stopped and stood, watching her.

She was standing there, illuminated by the light from the window: of average height, broad, wide-eyed, red-haired. She was wearing a white robe, a man's robe that looked big on her, one hand holding the hem while the other gently swirled a kanaka over a low flame. She smiled, as though expecting me.

"I'm Alya. Coffee?"

One slow nod and I had forgotten the world outside.

When, later, I'd try to remember the song Alya had been singing in the kitchen that morning I would fail, and when she told me she couldn't remember either, I'd tell myself that surely she must know, that she couldn't be trying hard enough. But I do recall the strange murmur she made as she was humming or breathing the tune; a sound as familiar as the faint rippling of the river beneath my feet. And I recall what she told me when I asked her what it was.

"*Haad*," she told me.

"*Haad?*"

"The sound of the sea."

Her mouth to my ear: "Close your eyes, Seif."

Her lips brushed my lobe and she hummed, and then there was the sound of waves surging. I could smell the sharp salt tang of my adolescence in Bahri. The days we used to take off up to Alexandria on the six a.m. train, trying to chat up pink peasant schoolgirls riding between their Delta towns—the girls crammed and jostling the length of the packed wooden benches, wedged against the broken windows—and at the end of the line, with the last of them gone, getting off at Sidi Gaber and taking the streetcar to Al Ramal.

"But it's not the same as *lajab*," she said.

"What's that again?"

"The sound of waves breaking against each other."

And then, to my astonishment, I heard the sound of the high crashing waves in whose clothes-soaking spray we used to delight. And I lifted my head, opened my eyes, and looked at her.

"What else?"

"Everything." She smiled. "All the sounds."

Himar: the sound of falling rain. *Ajij*: the sound of flame. Flutterings, tricklings, grazings, trillings. Sounds I didn't know had names, names I didn't know had sounds, and Alya knew every one, could sing them all. In the morning, humming; in the evening, singing; at midday taking me on a journey through the sounds of every wave there was.

But the word for the sound of the river over which we walked? That, I could not remember. I watched Bahr climbing a flight of steps on the far bank. He turned back to me and asked, "Are you ready to see more?"

5

A DOCTOR

The first thing Ashraf noted was the absence of mirrors. There were broad windows, their tinted glass blotting up the pale light, but no mirrors. There wasn't a single familiar face in this strange place, and he couldn't even see his own.

Ashraf had a young man's face despite the gray in his hair. Like the rest of his class, he had been in his mid-twenties when he'd finally graduated from medical school, followed by three years of national service, emerging within touching distance of thirty. Leaving camp on the last day of service, the desert highway leading to the camp had seemed to stand for the long bleak road that had been his life so far, then, as it stretched away, the longer journey yet to come: employment, further studies and qualifications, everything that sent a spasm through his colon when he thought of it.

Just to put food in his mouth he joined the

practice of a doctor who was an acquaintance of a former classmate. A clinic in a working-class neighborhood where he made a few pennies each month. It wasn't that his future looked black; rather, it had vanished into the distance some considerable time ago and there was no hope now of catching it.

When the offer came he hardly had to think about it at all.

They just told him it was a private clinic. Situated in a quiet neighborhood, only the best people as patients. He was eager, but wary; he couldn't understand why they would pick someone like him for such an evidently lucrative position. But when he arrived, there were surprises in store. The first was that the clinic was not located on a street or square, but within the walls of a villa, a palace: through the gates and down a long and verdantly fringed drive. The second was that the hospital had no name—what signs there were identified the different departments. The third surprise? Though it was full of people shuffling around in hospital whites, Ashraf didn't see a single patient; no one who so much as looked ill. Nor was there a cafeteria for visitors, or a reception area: it was like you skipped all the preliminaries and stepped directly into the heart of the hospital, and there the beds that filled its rooms were few, and empty.

At first, Ashraf told himself that perhaps the clinic hadn't opened to the public yet. Then he realized that not only had there been no opening, there never would be. No opening, no visitors, no patients. The entire place ran for the sake of just one man, and he wasn't even ill. The X-rays and diagnostic images hanging on the walls of the various departments all came from the same source: those radiographed teeth sat in his jaw; the kidney on the right of that digestive tract belonged to him. Even the lectures delivered in the modest medical institute annexed to the hospital, and the doctors who graduated from it: everything revolved around the workings and wellness of a single body.

There was nothing public about the place; it gathered no data, made no findings that might be more generally applied. This was not "a place of treatment"; it was a place for the treatment of Ibrahim Alalayli. Remove that name from the equation and you had nothing.

Ashraf encountered young doctors who had never studied or treated anything but the health and habits of Alalayli: orthopedists who'd straightened only Alalayli's bones; heart specialists who specialized in Alalayli's heart. Of all these generalists, surgeons, hematologists, and vascular experts only a small minority, very rarely, were actually compelled to make some intervention. Most would stay in the laboratory for years on end, studying and analyzing and running routine tests. There were those, like Ashraf, who'd arrived after a short stint in the field; others had only known the lecture hall. Some were skilled and respected practitioners who had retired but accepted Alalayli's proposal that they drop everything to care for him should the call come. Most worked in the building full time, a few lived there, and a very few actually traveled with him wherever he went. There was the car that carried the personal bodyguards and then, never more than a few meters away, another vehicle, unremarkable from the outside, but fitted out with state-of-the-art equipment and carrying a team of highly skilled doctors and paramedics. Never more than a few meters from their client, who wouldn't move an inch without them, sat the emergency room elite and the specialists—heart and veins and brains.

Alalayli had resolved not to die.

In time, the doctors at Alalayli's hospital came to believe they were incapable of treating any body other than their client's. It was simple enough to announce they'd retired or taken new jobs in distant provincial hospitals; the problem was with friends and relatives, casually requesting advice or calling up with medical emergencies. The real issue wasn't Alalayli's unbreakable rule, which stated that any doctor caught treating anybody other than him would be dismissed with extreme prejudice (the word *prejudice* being in no way metaphorical, since Alalayli had the means to exact revenge, to do damage, to imprison people if he so chose). No, the problem was that all the staff, Ashraf included, gradually came to feel that they were the property of Alalayli's hospital; or that, more precisely, they realized the one thing that made the idea of introducing their diagnoses and scalpels into the lives of ordinary people bearable, was the sheer range of these people, their diversity and profusion. It was this profusion that allowed a doctor to feel an error here might be put right there; gifted them the scrupulous equivocation of the soldier in an execution squad, who can't know if the fatal bullet is chambered in his gun or that of the man next to him. A doctor might legitimately wonder, did he kill the patient, or was it someone—something—else? But here, where there was only one patient, one life at stake, there was no washing your hands of responsibility, no escaping the knowledge that you'd killed.

Thoughts which filled his head as he made his way to and from the hospital, turning them over as he sat at his desk, reading up on the patient he might never see—he came to believe that these thoughts were his secret, and his alone. Trapped behind the walls of this silent, green-corridored palace, he felt like a stranger in the company of others.

But all that changed the day he heard whispers about a stranger in their midst. A young woman named Sherine who both belonged there and didn't. The rumors said that she was Alalayli's daughter. Then he saw her: flitting past him down the corridor, a bird barely touching to earth. To Ashraf, it seemed as if some ghostly breeze stirred her hair, lifting it out behind her. And as she neared the exit a thin young man stood up. He didn't seem to belong to her world at all, yet he followed her out.

The same whispers brought Ashraf the young man's name—Salaam—and his story.

6

A WHITE COW THE SIZE OF A HAND

Doctors who were believers astonished Bahr. Didn't they see the elephant in the room? Medicine's an atheist, he would say. By its very nature! How else to explain the errors in creation? The mistakes that stemmed from the source, bred into the bone—the faults in construction that prevent these bodies of ours from carrying their miserable tenants through even the handful of decades allotted to them?

"If a doctor *must* have faith," Bahr said, rolling a cigarette, "then it should be in his own divinity, in himself. He's spent a lifetime fixing this shoddy design, giving those creatures another, better chance at existence. Doctors' practices are licensed repair shops that honor the warranty on the products of Our Lord.

"If medicine isn't an atheist then there'd be no need to fight so hard against microbes and viruses, all those cells that suddenly turn on themselves. You

could fight half, a quarter, as hard and leave the rest
to God.

"That said," Bahr went on, "I *have* seen a god. I've
seen *many* gods abroad in this world. A young doctor
was the first, a woman I met not more than a month
after arriving in the land of ice and snow. I was hungry, without shelter. Seif, I would pick through the
garbage till I found something unspoiled to eat. But
Seif…their garbage! Finer than the food in half the
restaurants here. Only, that day I'd been unlucky, or
maybe the fault lay in this faulty body of mine. I had
eaten a doughnut which I'd found still wrapped in
white paper, just two bites taken from its edge; two little snips from—so I imagined—the pretty teeth of an
angel, like those that passed me on the street. So I ate
it, and my belly briefly quieted, but then this tremendous pain ignited inside me, like a dog was worrying
at my guts. The sweat was dripping off me, turning
instantly icy in the cold, and the world was spinning.

"I woke to the face of a god.

"She was leaning over me like the sky, smiling,
and talking to me in their language. I could hear
only heavenly sounds. Then she laid her milk-white
fingers on my shoulder and spoke in other tongues,
now in English and now in French, and I saw that I
was dressed in white, in a hospital gown, and all the
while this young doctor—she must have been in her
mid-twenties, no more—kept on talking to me and
smiling.

"It took some effort, but I managed to understand
that I'd been poisoned. Not by the delicious doughnut,

though; it was alcohol poisoning, from the bottle I'd taken from a semi-comatose homeless man down by the river. It would have killed me if the ambulance hadn't arrived and carried me off to this young doctor who first pumped my stomach, then, settling me down, smiled at me and insisted I stay put till morning.

"In the morning my clothes came, and I saw that they had been washed and folded, and when at last I left, I passed the doctor standing in a doorway, pale from her sleepless night. She gave me a tired smile. 'Goodbye, Mr. Bahr,' she said. I was feeling like myself again, feeling full, like I'd live for a thousand years, but this modest deity was content with a curt nod of acknowledgment. She wanted no thanks. She had cured me as I was dying, fed me when I was hungry, clothed me against fear, and not a word of thanks did she ask in return. If she'd ordered me to worship her I would have dropped to my knees. Nor was she the only god I met there.

"There was the old man and his wife who invited me for tea in their house—more of a shack, really. On the edge of a forest. Maybe it was a vacation house, I don't know. Do gods go on vacation? Do they work?

"Anyway, I was freezing. They gave me a cup of tea and offered me the use of a mattress on the floor of a small, warm room. They weren't afraid of me, and I didn't thank them, and when I went to sleep I dreamed that they were leaning over me. Perhaps they were.

"The next morning, they laid out a breakfast, which I duly ate, and then the old god spoke to me.

He told me that he believed in one religion and one devotion; that every day you help another human being. And he invited me to join him in this faith, but in those days I was a sinner, quite irredeemable, so I left them there and kept on running.

"This was years after my encounter with the god at the hospital. I had come to their paradise, committed a crime, and I was on the run. But the gods were everywhere."

As Bahr paused, we found ourselves approaching the wall that was our destination. An old temple wall, its reliefs worn smooth but still, with their ghostly traces, speaking of the site's original purpose.

Dawn was breaking as we climbed a rough track through thickets of scrub. We rose with the hillside, the Nile we had crossed like saints falling away behind us, broad and still and unobtrusive, its banks lined with a thin strip of palms and indeterminate foliage. Just as we were beginning to pant, there, suddenly, was an opening in the slope's rocky folds, scarcely large enough to let a grown man through, and in this opening, from within, fingers beckoned. So we bent and entered.

I had been expecting quiet, and the voices and blur of movement took me by surprise. When my eyes adjusted to the light I saw a large group seated on the ground, most of them women and children, and caught the scent of incense in the air. Overhead, the sun was rising shyly, preceded by its rays, which—an expertly placed spotlight—fell against a bright and almost blank white wall.

The singing began.

Praise songs for the Prophet, prayers, God's names—all sounded echoless and somehow out of keeping in this ancient space—and then the women and children fell silent, though their chants and charms continued to tremble in the air. Everyone was staring at the wall, as though they were at the movies, and I stared with them.

Here was the cure for those who were denied visions, for those whose supplications fell flat: the wall was the secret these clustered hamlets never divulged. To strangers, this was nothing but a scored and pillaged ruin, but for these people, for the few minutes between dawn and sunup on those blessed mornings following the full moon nights, you could, if a true believer and full of love, see the one you sought.

Look closely, then, and pray hard to the prophets, and when your faith is brimming over then you'll see them—the beloved dead. Clear as day or through a veil. Held by your eye or embodied in your mind. They will greet you or guide you or reassure you. Look at the wall until your eyes go white with it, till they blink and tear.

We began to hear muffled weeping around us, and the sound of the women murmuring names. As I sat there, cross-legged, a little boy crawled past my foot and I leaned forward to brush his hair—it startled me with its coarseness. Then I leaned back against the wall. I told myself that if these people were able to see their departed here, in this place, then surely so should I. And I stared until my eyes burned, and I saw.

I saw night and, in that night, the form of a black dog moving through the darkness. It was followed by a second dog, then a third, then two more until there were five. Five dogs standing on a street corner I thought I recognized, and now on the move, trotting quickly in formation toward the entrance to a building, like a military patrol. An entrance that made me sit up straight.

It was the apartment building I'd grown up in, my place of play and sanctuary. I saw the five dogs pad up the stairs to the fifth floor where we'd lived and pause for a moment outside our apartment, and then I heard the first dog howl, quickly joined by the others.

Then I remembered. I saw and I remembered.

I had been asleep in the living room when I was woken by the sound of someone calling my name. I saw my father's big dark body in its white vest emerge from his bedroom and walk to the front door. He peered through the peephole and recoiled, muttering in shock and surprise. Then, taking a deep breath, he threw the door open.

My father had thrown the door open and stood in the entryway of our apartment. Facing him, the five dogs, now silent. The leader had yawned, a final, unvoiced howl as though delivering a message, then had turned and padded down the stairs with the others following noiselessly behind.

We only understood the message a week later, when my mother died.

I felt my shoulder being gently shaken and I looked up to see Bahr, a smile of sympathy on his lips: "You slept?" This time, I didn't tell him what I had seen and he didn't ask. Looking around, I saw there were no women anymore, no children, no one. The deserted space was filled with sun, and by its bright light the temple seemed like a normal tomb; the carvings I'd thought pharaonic reduced to the idle scratchings of visitors.

As we were leaving, Bahr held a whispered conversation with the man who had beckoned us in earlier and seemed to hand him something—or was he taking it?—and then we were back on the path we'd climbed, the heat of the day penetrating our clothes and pricking us with sweat. As the ground leveled off, Bahr turned and started to go a different way than the one we'd come by, following the dictates of a scheme whose madness, at least, was becoming clearer to me with every passing day. From time to time I would watch him from the corner of my eye, and would be invaded by a sudden terror. The reality of my situation: I was in the company of a total stranger, in places that were quite isolated and strange to me.

Yet I was also a stranger to the person I had been just days earlier, that hot afternoon, when Leila approached me during one of her rare visits to the magazine and, an air of purpose about her, forbade me from opening my mouth. Then she produced from the magic box of her handbag the most unexpected object: a white ceramic cow the size of my palm. She handed it to me and said, "You have no excuse now," and gazed into my eyes with a strength that shook my heart and a smile I tried not to see. Then she delivered her double-edged command:

"Seif, wake up!"

Her statement—her order, rather—was meant literally. I'd assumed the thing would sound like a regular alarm clock, despite being done up to look like a grinning cow, but at the appointed time it lowed. A deafening low that snatched me quaking from sleep in order to silence the noise. It felt like it might break the windows. That such a small object could produce such a terrific din astonished me, and I was reminded of the surprise I'd received a few days before. The name Bahr Kamel was unusual. A man called Ocean suggested a bearlike figure—if not broad then very tall at least—but the man I met was more like short and thin. Short and thin and gray-haired, wearing the jeans and bright blue T-shirt of a younger man.

Leila told me he was waiting for me in the lobby. As soon as he saw me he slid elegantly to his feet, there was a brief introduction, then he took my arm and gently guided me to the exit so that we could continue our conversation outside. I was no stranger to monomaniacs barging into the office with bombshells that only ever burst in their own minds, but this man had none of that unbalanced energy and I went with him. Outside on the street, he glanced around, pulled a small notebook from his pocket, and, after a brief consultation, announced that the alley was nearby.

We crossed July 26 Street, then Tawfiqiya, and as we were approaching Ramses Street it seemed for a moment that we must be making for the train station, but he turned instead toward Galaa, along the green-painted railings and past the coffee shop that was famous for its poor service. Now I was sure we must be headed for a grand old historic building that lay up ahead, but before we reached it, Bahr stopped and smiled.

"Get ready."

He tucked the notebook back in his pocket, pulled his upturned collar tight around his neck, and strode quickly past the entrance to the old building. The building turned out to have a twin further down the street, and between the two was a long alley at whose far end could just be seen the yellow roofing of the train station. What surprised me, though, was the powerful ice-cold breeze that issued from it. Our clothes began to flap and beat, and I looked around to see where this wind might be coming from, but there was nothing to see except the silent marble walls, featureless but for little openings set high up, like the loopholes in the ramparts of a Mamluk fortress. Bahr produced a small camera and took a few shots, and then he pulled out a second device, pressing down on one side of it and waiting for a few moments, before returning it to his bag. He jotted a few words in his notebook and clutched at his flapping shirt. "Let's go," he said.

We retreated back to the street, me trailing behind in silent bewilderment, and as soon as we emerged from between the twin buildings we were once again pressed flat by the furnace heat of mid-July.

But after that first trip to the alley, Bahr had vanished, lost amid the ghosts who crowded ever thicker around me, and I almost forgot about him altogether. In fact, the thing I remember most clearly from that time was finding out that Leila had taken a team from the magazine to the scene of the gruesome accident that the press would dub "the elevator children"—a case whose surreal and bloody details were received with horror by a captivated nation.

And then a few days after hearing this news, I saw her again. She was back in the editor's office, leaning against the wall beside the low window, but rather than looking out at the street or up at the sky she was looking straight down, as though examining her shoes. I was able to watch her for a moment before she noticed me, at which point she said, without preamble, "They made us walk over corpses." I thought how much she'd changed. I caught myself staring at her legs as they rose up into her skirt, and I imagined them—those legs—walking over me. And when I realized that this made me a corpse, I thought that I didn't much care.

I had dreamed of her the night before. A few nights before, maybe. We were sitting together, at home, and eating macaroni that Leila had cooked; the same recipe we used to order from a small restaurant in Bab Al Louq back when we first met. The food smelled and tasted delicious, and I knew that soon we'd be headed for the bedroom, and there was this sudden access of joy. But as Leila turned away from me to get up and fetch a glass of water, I felt a hair in the food in my mouth. Quickly, before she came back and caught me, I pulled at it. It was long and red, from a woman's head, and it kept on coming, longer and longer, endlessly long. I began to choke. I remember choking and pulling and glancing up wretchedly in anticipation of Leila's return. Then the dream ended.

Leila brought me back to reality: "You're going to accompany him on an expedition. The magazine's sending you."

I stared at her uncomprehendingly, and she smiled in disbelief.

"Bahr! Don't you remember him?"

I watched as she slipped behind her desk and sat down. So confident, as though she'd been here forever. There was something astonishing about the way she'd managed to make herself at home. But I knew this train of thought would bring me pain, and I shut it down. Instead, I thought to myself how difficult it was to guess Bahr's age.

"An expedition? Where?"

"Here," she said, pointing to the floor. "Egypt, I mean."

I had no choice. I couldn't refuse. It had been a while since I'd submitted a piece of any consequence and had it not been for Leila taking pity on me and interceding on my behalf I would have been fired long ago. I'd stopped being surprised by Leila's capacity for sudden interventions, the fact that she was saving me even though it was me who had introduced her to the magazine. To journalism, in fact… Once again, I shut the thought down.

I had been told that Bahr was an Egyptian who had returned home after several years living abroad, and that he—or so he claimed—was in the process of researching a long, serialized piece on a list of selected sites in Egypt, with a book in mind, maybe. The magazine wanted me to accompany him, and this was the plan:

Bahr was going to write up detailed dispatches on his expeditions to be published in the country of his former exile, and I would write for our magazine: reports on Bahr and his project. Quite a challenge for someone like me, who didn't get around much and hadn't cared about anything for years.

"Isn't there anyone else? Someone who'd actually enjoy this kind of thing?"

"Lots of people," she snapped. Then, after a pause: "It was Bahr who chose you, not the magazine."

There was an astonished silence.

"Don't ask me why. Maybe you could ask him yourself."

I stared at her, the color drained from my face. I'd only met the man once and my name wasn't well known enough to have caught the attention of an Egyptian overseas. The only way it would have gotten there is if I'd sailed ahead of it. Then, perhaps because Bahr did seem to know me and had requested me by name, a faint enthusiasm began to glow and catch inside me. Fearing any response that might douse this thin flame—yet more disappointment for Leila and myself—I shrank from seeking an explanation.

A job that might get me out of my rut, I told myself, and then, however many days or weeks later, I could return to my bed and Bahr could go back into exile. Who knows, maybe it would make it possible for me to go overseas. It might clear a path to lead me back to Leila. Or her to me.

Even before I knew the details, I had started to picture the assignment—this chain of investigations that has brought me this present moment. And everything I imagined, like everything else in life, turned out to be pure fantasy.

Slowly but surely I would come to understand that the whole edifice of articles and reports were cover for something else entirely, something considerably crazier—if we might be permitted to divide the world along those lines: the crazy and the not—but back then I didn't know that. Nor did I know (and neither, somehow, did Bahr) that we would not be coming back. Just as had happened to Alya, before us.

Ahead of me, Bahr descended the shallow slope away from the way we'd come, mopping at his brow and calling out that our next stop was the village. The village of the departed. A place whose inhabitants had all died, I assumed, or been dispersed among the country's towns and cities. The truth, like everything on this expedition, turned out to be stranger still. But before he could tell me more, I felt courage enter me and, suddenly buoyed, I called Bahr's name. When he turned, I asked the question my pride had long deferred: "Why me?"

7

HER SINGER

What if you were able, somehow, to travel back to the very beginning of time, and then began to draw up a comprehensive taxonomy of all discoveries: a list of what came about by pure chance and what was the product of deliberate application and dedicated research? Two lists, then. On which, do you think, would you find the sciences, or theories? Where would the name of this artist be, or that football player? What about these territories and islands and mines, these emotions and betrayals? Which list would claim civilization? The wretchedness of the human condition?

Salaam, the singer—if he might be allowed to describe himself as such—could not make up his mind. He couldn't even decide on which of the two lists his own discovery might fall. The initial discovery of his voice had been his and his alone, which may have been why he thought of it as his secret. He didn't have the courage to sing in front of others, only to himself, so he had no idea whether his voice was truly sweet or whether it was all in his mind.

He developed a stutter when he was young. His mother sought out special schools and therapists, but in vain, and he had continued to stutter and stammer to the amusement of his classmates and exasperation of his teachers until, at last, he had withdrawn into himself, his lesson learned: don't speak.

Only when he spoke to himself—in himself—did that inner tongue unknot and free. Once, breathing along to a song on the radio, he nearly convinced himself that voice was beautiful, after all. And then he smiled: Don't we all feel that way? Another time, feeling bold, he sang in front of the mirror, as though he might catch sight of the song issuing from between his lips. Once again he took pleasure in his voice, and once again he smiled. And then he stopped, astonished.

His surprise had nothing to do with the loveliness of his voice, it was that the words of the song had flowed out of him without a break: no stammer, unfumbled. Like he was a professional singer. Better yet, like he was any other ordinary young man, just singing a tune. And for the first time he felt that he was a human being. He couldn't have said why, but the very next thing that came to his mind was love. So he stopped singing and for a brief moment, closed his eyes. He opened his mouth and began to speak to the mirror, to talk, but almost immediately fell silent again. The stutter had returned. He drew a breath and sang, and again that enchanting river of a voice.

Then he spoke and the stutter was back. He banged his hand on the rim of the sink beneath the mirror and let out a stutter of despair.

At work, sitting with his colleagues at lunch, he plucked up his courage and decided that now was the time: he would sing or—to be more exact—would murmur a song. The first two words came out naturally enough—*fakkarouni izzay*—and when everyone turned around in astonishment, he sang louder: *huwaaana nseeee eetet seet see...* The stutter was back, a sucker punch, and a shout of laughter went up, followed by an embarrassed hush. Someone patted him on the shoulder and they changed the subject. At the end of the break they all went back to their desks.

He spent the night awake: running a temperature, writhing in the sheets.

He felt he would never recover that courage. He became a man who stayed out late and drank. Then, one evening, alone at the bar, under the cover of low lighting and the crowd of drinkers, he murmured a tune and he heard a woman say, "You have a beautiful voice."

He turned. She was as bewitching as she'd sounded, and from the very first he knew she would not be his.

"Go on," she said; his courage climbed out of its grave, and there, to his bewilderment, was his voice, as exquisite and smooth and unbroken as when he'd stood alone before the mirror.

8

THEY DIDN'T LOOK BACK

At first we saw a figure, someone hiding behind a wall and peering around the corner, but when we drew near we realized that the someone was a rag. A scrap from a robe, perhaps, caught on the wall and flapping back and forth in the breeze like a little flag.

At the entrance to the village were the remains of a coffee shop—closer to a roadside stall: two wooden benches beneath a tree and a palm-fiber rope slung on the ground around them to create the illusion of inside and outside. Our feet disappeared into a mist of garbage through which small, unidentifiable creatures moved about. I tensed, but took solace from my sturdy boots and Bahr's unruffled calm.

He'd responded to my question by promising that he would explain why he'd chosen me, and everything else as well, once we came to the final stop on our journey. Recalling the foreboding I'd felt the day Leila entrusted me with this job, I didn't press him further.

Once past the wall with its rag and the deserted stall, the houses came into view.

We were a long way from the highway and not a living sound came from the village—the silence was absolute. Unsettling to a city boy. We were in the Delta, but the houses were built tall, in the southern style, and perhaps it was only because I knew we were close to the sea, but I caught the tang of iodine and salt in the air. The houses where we strolled smelled of nothing at all.

Doors ajar or flung wide, and beyond them, by the light of the moon, nothing but shadowed walls and a dusting of debris on dirt floors: an article of clothing, pages from a notebook, empty packets and peels. The sound of my footsteps answered Bahr's like an echo as we approached a door that seemed to beckon us inside. Tentatively, we entered.

It was just two rooms with a black pit in one corner that we took to be the toilet. I thought I heard a sound, a whisper close by, but when I turned around there was nothing and no one. Nothing, not even a broken chair or a smashed cup; it was as though an atom bomb had turned everyone and everything to vapor.

As always, Bahr started scribbling and recording and photographing, while I stood there trying—and failing—to visualize the events that had led to this scene.

Wahda.

Residents of neighboring villages had failed to notice that the inhabitants of Wahda were selling everything they owned. Literally: from their scant livestock and chickens to clothes—down to underwear—dropped off at second-hand stalls and rag sellers; from the cheapest of cheap shoes and worn-through flip-flops to treasured television sets and cellphones. Trucks and taxis were disposed of at a considerable loss.

Wherever they went, they were circumspect and discrete in the execution of their plan, trying not to draw attention to themselves. Children were cautioned not to talk to strangers; the men in their gatherings smoking hashish and the women at market were instructed to hold their tongues.

Wahda was a small village, very small. Closer, in fact, to a hamlet. When one of Wahda's prodigal sons returned from a lengthy sojourn in Italy—Hagg Ashraf's son, Salem, carried home on the waves, having swallowed half the Mediterranean and sickened on its burning salt—it wasn't long before he was dazzling any friends and neighbors he could find with his tales of far-off lands: countries where there is no oppression, no hunger, no bribery, no officers to humiliate you or smack the back of your neck or lock you up on a whim. All that they'd heard before, of course, in similar tales from overseas. What truly dazzled them, what got them dreaming, was that Salem was now an organizer of the fabled trans-oceanic trips. At last, the village had its own accredited representative to charm them out of the genie's lamp of woe and starvation in which they lay slumped; a key to free them from their timeless poverty. Now, they could send their children abroad—could even join them there, if they wanted.

In fact, parents were shouldering their own offspring aside in their haste to get to Salem, bargaining and swearing oaths of kinship and friendship in pursuit of a discount. Then they began to compete, brother against brother, neighbor against neighbor, calling in loans and arguing over who would travel this trip and who the next. Then Salem came to them with an extraordinary offer.

He told them that he could offer a significant discount on his rate, putting the trip within reach of anyone who wished to go, but on the condition they provide him with four hundred committed travelers, all to be conveyed in a single boat (whose owners he described as "new to the trade"). He wouldn't be forced to rent any more boats from the big-time smugglers, and a reduced rate could be had.

Did Salem mean what happened to happen from the outset, or was he simply trying to get as many on board as he could? Hard to say, but there were hasty, whispered consultations, an exchange of knowing glances, one last check with a young man's legal guardian, and Wahda came to its decision: They'd all go together; the whole village.

Parents and children, grandfathers and grandmothers, men and women and suckling babes; all of them would leave. "In a little place like Wahda…" they said, "In a tiny little place like Wahda, just forty-two households all told, which is to say…" (everyone fell silent, computing hard) "…four hundred and sixteen souls, we can't leave some behind while the rest sail away. We'll travel as one."

By the date they were due to depart, six births and three deaths had brought their number to four hundred and nineteen. With all their possessions sold, they had spent the last few nights sleeping on the ground. They had agreed to meet in Balteem and so set out: some on foot, others in vehicles. The last to leave the village destroyed the little signpost, which the village letterer had painted just two months before his death. They threw the sign down and heaped it with dust. Like burying the place's history; wiping its memory clean away. Little village of poverty, of hunger, of forgetting: farewell.

The boat came through the fog at dawn. They moved through the scattered tin shacks tucked between the dunes of Balteem and emerged, clans and families, brothers and sisters and aunts and cousins, to clamber slowly into the sea-dark boat, whose prow dipped at each boarding to sip the waves, then rose. On deck, they assembled family alongside family, clan next to clan, their distribution on board a map of the homes they'd left behind; the North, South, East, and West of their modest rural district. They brought nothing with them, just a little food and water, though a few girls held tiny dolls constructed from rabab frames, doum husks, and locks of hair.

The village had clambered in and—every soul accounted for, rope cast off, anchor raised, oars rolling—slipped away into the dark. Not one of them would ever again so much as think of Wahda, where Bahr and I now stood.

9

NOBODY NOTICED THINGS HAD CHANGED

It irritated me, the constant fidgeting of the thin young man who sat between us, his knee knocking a tattoo against the table leg. Just a short while later, I was to stop holding anything against him, but at that particular moment, there in the café, I could not meet his eye without betraying my agitation. He was telling us the story of what had happened to their building.

It was when the building's elevator suddenly stopped working that the residents first really understood the danger posed by the construction of the new hotel next door. Vast excavators and dozers disrupted the pipes and wiring that fed into their venerable building. The electricity started cutting out: the wooden elevator gave up the ghost, appliances fell silent, exploding lightbulbs were a daily ritual. But this wasn't the worst of it.

They had expected someone would turn up to negotiate or kick the doors down and try to throw them out. Theirs was the last building on the street whose residents had not stepped aside for some office block or hotel or new bank. They were mainly middle-class families, those branches that drooped from affluence until they brushed the dirt. Their apartments had been inherited from respectable parents and bourgeois grandparents, along with the fixed rent, to whose modest demands their lives were so habituated that they were no longer able to sell up and move. When construction began on the hotel, they'd said, "Our chance has come. They'll try to tempt us with a payoff. Maybe even upgrade the building. It's happened before!"

Neither one nor the other.

They were ringed by enormous machinery, bulldozers and cranes, the engineers in white helmets, the laborers in yellow, smashing the street to pieces and blocking traffic, and then there was the construction work itself: endless shifts through day and night to raise up "The Largest Hotel in the Middle East." Elevators full of workmen floated up and down past their apartments; there was the sense that the men inside might step onto their balconies and join them for breakfast if they left their windows ajar. It felt, in fact, as though the few meters which separated their building from the hotel's wall had been erased; like they were now at the heart of things. At night, beams from great floodlights cut through the tinted glass and blackout curtains in their bedrooms. Cranes shook their walls. Sleep became impossible. Even conversation was a burden.

And no one acknowledged their complaints. Next to the billionaire funders of this colossal undertaking they were ants.

Gradually, they became conscious that a neurosis was taking hold: even away from the building the machine din filled their minds. Their problems multiplied: at work, with family, out on the street, and in the cafés. None of them could hold their temper in an argument, could tolerate a single word of disagreement, the slightest skeptical sound. The building's children fought with their classmates at school and in daycare. Those residents who were managers became more tyrannical, the young women lost patience with their lovers, mothers with sons, and everyone grew used to shouting just to make themselves heard. During the very brief moments when the construction halted or the electricity cut out, passers-by would hear raised voices from the building's balconies and windows: the voices of grown men and women, of children, of the elderly, seemingly in perpetual dispute. But if they listened carefully, they would have realized that these were perfectly inoffensive conversations bellowed at top volume. The few remaining inhabitants of the rapidly emptying residential building on the other side of the construction site went out of their way to avoid interacting with the neurotics. You could pick them out at a distance: the pecking stride, the darting eyes, the fingers which, close inspection revealed, were always trembling.

All this was true, yet visitors to the building tended to find the inhabitants' complaints overblown.

Initially, at least. In those first moments the din seemed fine. Soon, though, the visitor would begin to sense it emanating from inside them—from their own middle ear perhaps: a growling hum that came from nowhere, it began pitched low and unobtrusive but in mere minutes the body was overrun. Like a dentist's drill, its point pushing into you forever and ever and ever.

We felt it, too, the day the young man took us—Bahr and I—to the building, then up to his apartment on the top floor. It was the day before we would walk on water. We stepped into an entrance redolent of a former grandeur, climbed a spiraling, high-ceilinged staircase, and no sooner were we seated than the building's muffled tremor began to claim us.

At first, like music. Like rock: powerful drum-beats on the gates of our consciousness, driving the body into motion, but a clenched and terrified motion, as though in self-defense. All around us the machines shuddered, so the ground shuddered and the old building's foundations with it. Then the shudder moved, crept over the floors and up the walls, shuddering the beds and chairs and cupboards, the gas ranges and the sinks on the wall. And all this at an intensity too slight for the naked eye to see or the flesh to feel, its frequency low as low can be—passing through pores and setting veins and arteries trembling, swaying the limbs in opposite directions, prompting an uproar within, denying sleep, even rest, to each and every living being—which is to say, to every human, the stray cats having long been driven from their perches on the staircase.

Every human except one man, that is. It was as though he'd been searching for a building just like this. He showed up one day as part of a team investigating the complaints and said (he and his colleagues said) that they did not themselves hear any sound at the volumes reported, but that (confronted with the residents' fury) they would make sure their superiors heard (the fury not the sounds). A few days later, the man was back, not to resolve the problem but to inquire, to their astonishment, whether there was an apartment to rent in the building.

And he did indeed take an apartment, paying its lucky owner enough so that he could live elsewhere while the young man moved in among them. Whenever they asked, he'd say that the complaint was taking its course. Other times he'd insist they be patient until the construction work was complete. Sometimes they'd be angry with him, sometimes they'd be conciliatory: he was their only entrée to the local council after all. Some of them realized, though, that his story might have been the strangest of all, even stranger than theirs.

When he told it to us—this young man who'd brought us up to his apartment—we were so astonished that for a few, brief moments we quite forgot the tremors that shook us as if we were on a train endlessly readying to depart.

10

THE SOUNDS OF THE WORLD WITHOUT EXCEPTION

– OR –

MY RED GLASSES

We were descending the dirt slope away from the empty village, the sun now a clear-cut fact in the sky. We went on away from the main road, the way it was in Bahr's plan, whose secrets he still kept close. Up a rise onto high ground dusted with green. Further up still, stones looked down on the silent dwellings, and we realized that these must be the graves.

The stones were low and scattered over the wilderness. There seemed to be far more of them than homes below, which seemed reasonable enough: the houses held—or had—the living, but the graves would hold the bones of everyone who'd lived here since the first hut went up.

We drifted slowly through the graves. Without close inspection I could barely make out the lettering in the stone, and from our elevated vantage point the Nile was just a pale blue line. We sat down to rest, and with no shade to be found, balanced our notebooks on our heads.

I remember that moment clearly, sitting in the company of unknown ancestors, because it was the first time Bahr told me anything about his past.

We had gone to see my grandmother. Me, my father, my mother. I mean, we'd gone to see her grave. The family tomb, I mean. Our graves aren't holes in a desert marked with stones, like the villages do out here; they're walled compounds, like the mausoleums in Cairo. My family's tomb has two rooms, one for the bones of the men, the other for the women. Anyway, we got to the tomb, and for some reason I started thinking of my friend Yasser who'd passed away years before. He used to play with us, though all the kids knew he was sick and so tried—at least most of us tried—not to do anything to upset him. But we were never sure how he was sick exactly. What the problem was. You'd be playing, and in the middle of a game, just like that, he'd slump to the ground and clutch his chest, his voice turning thin as a steam whistle. Then one day, without warning, he wasn't playing with us anymore. Next thing we knew, he was dead. He was some kind of relative, so they put him in our tomb.

To my parent's surprise I walked straight past the entrance to the women's chamber and into the men's, and there I stood and said a prayer for him, shy as a little boy. Once I'd rejoined them my father asked me, smiling, "So who got the prayer?"

"Yasser," I said.

My father, still smiling: "You could pray for him anywhere."

"So why do we come here for Grandma?"

"To keep her company. So she can hear us and see us."

"Same for Yasser, then."

My father shook his head and patted mine, but then Sayyid, son of Umm Sayyid the caretaker, dropped his bomb:

"Yasser's not here. We cleared the tomb out six months ago."

The first I'd ever heard of clearing tombs. I was told that whenever the tomb grew too crowded with bones, they were gathered up and interred far away, in the cliff face.

I was shocked. Why the tomb, then? Why build a tomb and guard a tomb? Why burial rites and burial shrouds if our ultimate fate is a hole in the cliff face? Why not bury us there in the first place if the tomb won't hold us longer than it takes to crowd with bones?

Which is why, once I grew older, I became so taken with the idea of cremation and scattered ashes.

From dust to dust. What need is there for a tomb, for a gravestone, for a shrine? Laid in a room alongside people you'd never liked until someone comes to clear you out. I've since learned that a body's cells are perpetually renewing. Like: I'm no longer the child who stood astonished in that tomb, nor am I the shy teenager at school, nor the adventurer I was as a young man, always risking death. The pair of red glasses I've owned for twenty years are older than any single scrap of my flesh, and they belong to me more surely than my nose or foot.

We rose in silence, the gravestones all around us and between us like stone shrubs, and I recalled an old tale I'd heard about the dead: that after their visitors leave they venture out and sit, backs against their gravestones, and talk. I remembered the day a spirit seemed to take possession of Alya; like, all of a sudden, her tongue was talking out of a former life that still inhabited her body.

That night I learned just how far away she had been born.

We were sitting out on the veranda of a restaurant that seemed completely untouched by what was going on in the world outside: still, soft-lit, the air conditioner bringing breezes that were scented like they'd passed through a garden of flowers. Her phone rang. Raising her hand in apology she answered the call, and then there she was, suddenly speaking a strange language, one I'd never heard before. I nearly choked on my food from the shock of it. As if a spirit had possessed her. Then she was smiling, a flower opening, as she passed me a glass of water.

I watched her until she finished the conversation, still smiling at the astonishment in my eyes. She said, "I was born at the ends of the earth."

An Asian country. Her father had been posted there. She and her sister had a habit of using the language whenever there were strangers around. But was the stranger someone next to her sister on the other end of the line, or was it me?

I hadn't yet understood the full, astonishing extent of Alya's talent for singing sounds. That these were no mere imitations: she *sang* the sound. Say, when she made a wave: her lips spilled a song of the sea so pure the wave itself would seem like the knock-off. I didn't grasp the wonder of it, I mean, until I discovered that her abilities were not confined to the quotidian soundscape—the sea, the rain, the wind; her miracle went further still.

We were sitting on cane chairs, tucked away in a park off one of Maadi's bijou public squares. We were both reading, and she was singing softly as she read, when all of a sudden I heard a sound I felt I knew, an astonishingly familiar sound, and I lifted my eyes and looked around. It was her. She was whistling, an odd little whistle out of which emerged, in no time, the clear sound of a breeze passing through an open window. I'd once had an apartment in one of a pair of identical towers that faced each other across the river, and this was the exact sound I used to hear on winter nights. The river on those nights took on an asphalt gray, while the asphalt of the corniche, agleam with rain, looked like the river. The ash-tinged clouds were so close they seemed to touch the tops of the towers. Most of the windows on the two highest floors were damaged from the wind's constant battering, and the air passing through the cracks made a sound exactly like the whistle now issuing from between Alya's lips in this out-of-the-way park in Maadi.

For the first time, I asked her what she did for a living. I'm ashamed to say that I'd assumed she lived off family money. With her sweet loopiness, her lightheartedness, her utter disregard for whatever life would bring, it had never occurred to me that she might work for a living. When I found out, I couldn't keep from smiling. It was as though everything suddenly clicked into place. Alya did voice work for animations. Not the childish squeaks of the characters themselves, but the sound effects—like crumpling tinfoil for footsteps through dry grass, or striking matches to give the impression of a fire igniting. Well, when they wanted particular sounds, harder, weirder, vaguer sounds, and didn't know what to do—when they wanted sandgrouse beating their wings through a stand of palms, or fruit rolling off the back of a truck on the highway, or sea foam licking the ears of a man just saved from drowning—then they turned to Alya.

I couldn't dream of a more perfect job for Alya's peculiar gifts. It came so naturally to her, so happily. And strange to say, I never failed to pick out Alya's true voice through a soundtrack's sonic mulch, her everyday pitch of conversation, argument, and love. It was a voice whose depth and warmth and clarity transmitted it directly into your head. Later, I asked her the question she'd no doubt had to answer a hundred thousand times before: "Why aren't you a professional singer?"

But she had no interest in being just another singer. She was, and I don't blame her, sufficiently enthralled with her own unique, almost unreal abilities. Dazzled by my discovery—perhaps because of the magical world which it revealed to me—I found myself unable to tell Alya about the thing that had, at one point, placed my whole future in jeopardy. What stopped me? Pride or fear or shame? Whatever the reason, I was reluctant to reveal a secret that would have to be revealed eventually and that, eventually, was revealed, though by then a lifetime had gone by and everything had changed. But even though I couldn't tell her, it was always on my mind:

When the editor called me in my heartbeat doubled. Exhausted by the hard years I'd traveled to this moment, yet here was the finish line at last! My head was held high or, if not actually high, then certainly not bowed. In the hush of the waiting room, his secretary smiled: "Go in."

Through the door and my shoes were lost in the thick carpet. I patted my back pocket to check my wallet and ID were there, wishing I'd brought a pen. I was telling myself he wouldn't mind if I had to borrow one of his, when there he was, smiling back at my smile and asking me to sit.

I waited for him to take the contract from a drawer, but he just went on smiling and said, "Congratulations." He asked me to confirm one last time that I wasn't currently under contract with any other company or agency, to which I shook my head vigorously. He nodded his as though this was the answer he'd expected. I grew concerned that the sound of my heartbeat would reach his huge ears. "Delighted you'll be contributing to the next issue," he said.

I said nothing, just nodded, and he went on:

"As you know, we get our share of scrutiny since we're not afraid to point the finger of blame. They try to bring us down, but because we know we are acting only in the best interests of our nation, we place our faith in Almighty God and press on."

I kept quiet and he kept talking.

"But God is the cause of causes."

He lit a cigarette.

"We've decided to make the next issue like…like a great cry, a cry great enough to strike dumb all those who accuse us of treachery and incitement."

I stared at him in amazement, watching his lips as they shaped these ringing words. "We'll outmaneuver them, and at the same time, we'll be scrupulously fair to those that deserve it. Now, I don't have to tell you this, of course. You've seen it for yourself: despite all their insinuations and instigations, we have *never*, not *once*, as God's our witness, *ever* received orders over the phone or from *anywhere else*, and we've *never* had an issue pulled or canceled."

He blew out smoke.

"And people have to understand this, too—that those who choose to protect us, out of the generosity of their hearts, well…they deserve to have us return the favor."

Three fingers were now extended, one after the other:

"We make our friends happy, we frustrate our

enemies, and we press on. Three birds with one stone. What's a harmless bit of flattery measured against the freedom we've been afforded all these years? Now, next week will be the birthday of the president—the president who's never forced us to write a single word or stripped so much as a letter from our pages—and of course everyone will be expecting us to break step with the blind loyalty of those other rags… But we'll surprise them; we'll be the most appreciative of the lot."

At last he got to his point, "Every journalist at this magazine is going to write an open letter to the president on the occasion of his birthday. That's the issue, the whole thing: open letters that outdo one another in their patriotism. It'll shut our enemies' mouths.

"This next issue is going to make us the subject of a lot of bewilderment, praise, and scorn. I'm expecting you, Seif, with all your talents, to offer up the loveliest flower in this garden of devotion. To take responsibility.

"Two days and I want your contribution on my desk. Brilliant as I'm sure it will be. The best of the bunch. And after we've celebrated, after we've had a chance to unwind and enjoy the fruits of our labors, management—and this is a promise, mind you, a certainty—will have finished drawing up new contracts, and yours will be at the top of the pile."

He took a breath. Smiled.

"Thank you, Seif."

Out I went, barely aware I was walking. I found myself standing at the window where I would later watch Leila. Unlike her, though, I wasn't looking at my feet, but at a tree down below whose leaves were stirring in a breeze. I looked at its branches, black in the night, and wondered why anyone would ever want to throw a stone at a harmless little bird; and what its chances of survival would be.

A bird of a type I couldn't identify flew over Bahr and me. The gravestones had finally petered out. We had yet to see another human.

11

ACCORDING TO PREFERENCE

"Dignity is the heaviest thing in a man," Bahr said as we waited for the doctor whose name, according to Bahr, was Ashraf. We weren't sitting in a waiting room, but in the cafeteria of a gas station by a highway on the outskirts of Cairo. "He's nervous," Bahr had told me. "He insisted we meet here."

"Dignity!" he said again. "It weighs about eighty kilos. A little less, perhaps."

He sipped at his coffee.

I was just a teenager when I found out. There was a protest in our town, about what I don't recall, and in the front ranks of the crowd I saw Soha. I'd seen her before at the state cultural institute and I'd liked what I saw, but I'd never plucked up the courage to talk to her. Really, what I'd liked were her legs, which had been on show to just below the knee. Rare enough in our little town. It was Soha's legs that taught me that

I was a lover of women's legs, those wings which hold their lovely bodies aloft. Not so fond that it could be called a fetish, mind you, but it certainly fit my personality: hesitant and wary the way all leg men are, in contrast to the stolid conservatism of the ass lover, the impetuousness of those who choose breasts. Later, I'd come to understand that the true taxonomy of men doesn't break down by star sign or ethnicity or geography, but rather a generally unacknowledged system of such preferences. Masochists are a guild of their own, stumbling in the darkness, sadists another, and so on, but long before I learned this, the way it all worked, there was only Soha's legs, which obsessed me and lured me to take part in a protest, despite lacking the courage to approach either her or the protestors. Then the police mounted a surprise attack and we all ran. I was still callow, so while the protest's leaders timed their escape to perfection, I kept delaying my retreat, and they caught me easily. A policeman started running after me. Since I was skinny I assumed I'd easily outpace his bulk, but then a second cop appeared in front of me, sprinting straight at me, and he balled his fist and caught me with it, right in the eye: his momentum plus mine. I was on the ground instantly, screaming, with all the darkness in the world gathered in the dead center of my eye and my eyelid like a wild beast had torn at it.

I came to in the dark: a vile stench, difficulty breathing, my body hemmed in. Like I was surrounded by bodies, but I couldn't make anybody out. Minutes went by, hours maybe, then I had what I'd subsequently identify as my first-ever panic attack. I've been on the brink of death often enough since, but nothing, not even death, compares to these attacks: the trembling, the inability to breathe, the feeling that you're toppling into an abyss while standing still.

They left us there. No food, no drink, nothing but that repulsive smell.

After I don't know how long, they called my name. I got to my feet—somewhere between terror and faint hope. At the door they made me take off my shirt, then blindfolded me with it and tied my hands behind my back.

I walked blind through sudden sounds and blows, mocking warnings to watch out for the wall, for open drains beneath me. After a while—after walking and climbing and going downstairs without passing through another doorway the whole time—I was ordered to get down, to squat. One of them pushed down on my shoulder. I tried leaning my back against the wall which I imagined must be there, only to meet a kick which stood me back upright. And it was there that I started to hear the voices. Female voices, high-pitched, crying out in exhaustion and fear. And among them, I heard Soha.

I threw my head around like a madman until one side of my blindfold slipped down and I saw them: three, maybe four young women, clinging to each other in terror, and Soha's face among them, bobbing in and out of sight. I watched as the scum searched them, or pretended to: hands that appeared to go into pockets and bags pushed instead between thighs and over breasts. For an instant the fear froze me, then I screamed.

"You sons of bitches!"

At least, that's what I meant to say, only what came out wasn't words but a lowing, and immediately the kicks rained in on my sides, the blindfold was yanked back up, and I was taken in to be interrogated.

But what do you care about the interrogation, Seif? It was an interrogation: meaningless questions in the darkest darkness; blows from behind, from everywhere. That held no surprises for me—it was what came after…

When, at last, they brought me home—once I'd learned the first truth that confronts all political prisoners when they are released (that after the warm embraces, the family's joy evaporates to leave a residue of silent reproach for all the fear you've put them through)—and when, after a momentary hesitation, I had gone back to the cultural institute, and had run into Soha, my spirit at last took flight. Brimming with the bravery of a man embarked on an adventure, I walked up to her and held out my hand.

She said, "Good to see you."

"It's good to see you, too," I replied.

Then I smiled, "We've paid our dues."

She stared at me. "What are you talking about?" she said.

Then her boyfriend came over. I gave him a "Good to see you," and they were gone.

Seif, I've never been sure whose voice I heard in

that corridor; what face it was I saw. I mean, maybe I mistook somebody else for her, because I was looking at a face, not the legs. Regardless, the point is that it was in that police station I learned that dignity has a specific weight—somewhere between seventy or eighty kilos.

Before they let us go, they took us out the back door of the cellblock into this dirt yard. They stripped us naked, or half-naked, and made us lie down on our stomachs. I didn't dare turn to look at the others. An officer came and put his shoe on my neck, then let his whole weight bear down on me till my face was crushed into the dirt. Like a mountain. Like there was a camel or a truck driving over me, driving me into the ground. There were tears in my eyes, and through the tears I saw a tiny insect crawling along by my nose, and then this fat fly came and settled right on the insect's back, and I... It was like the fly was staring at me out of two big blue eyes. My mother used to say that the flies that fly close to the ground are the spirits of our ancestors, and at that moment I fully believed it. I was convinced it was going to speak to me. The officer's weight on my neck was getting lighter, though he didn't get off, and it was then that I had a realization, like a revelation. The weight on my neck wasn't the officer, pulled to earth by gravity and crushing me in between. This was my dignity: seventy or eighty kilograms. It was puppy fat: the dignity I was yet to use up, and the time had come to let it fly away in the company of that departing fly. So I let my nose be crushed into the dirt, and I let my

---

neck turn slack like sponge, and I made an alliance with that oh-so-tiny insect, crawling along now by my eye: "You and me, together in the dirt, but you carry no dignity with you, no false dreams, no anger. You live and die without philosophy, as we all should. Hook my dignity out through my nose, little friend, and take it away. Help me bleed it out so I can be as weightless as you."

An odd contentment passed over me, like the breeze, and I felt that I was the ground itself, that I was a bank of dust across which the officer's weight was now distributed, unmoved and unaffected.

Then the stench that hung around the place prompted another revelation. You can never make a living room out of a bathroom.

Look around, Seif, look at the wide world around you, and picture it as one enormous house. You've got your living room and your hallway, bedrooms and a kitchen, a roof and stairs, maybe even a basement or storage room. And there are bathrooms, too, and in these bathrooms are toilets and drains. These drains…no matter how pretty you make them, how much you dress them up, they're still drains. Anyone who dreams of turning a bathroom into a living room is crazy, and crazier if they attempt it.

So it was, under the effects of the inspiration that came to me beneath the officer's shoe, I resolved that, should I live, should I ever get out from under, I would quit this toilet. I would leave it all behind and go to other countries, to other lands, and revel in their variety. For this one, say, is like a living room, warm and welcoming, and that country is a window, made to gaze out of, and another is a garden—a paradise by day and inky black at night—and then there's one that is a corridor, only good for passing between two more. The point was, you never go back to the toilet, unless…

I finished it for him: "Unless to shit?"

Bahr smiled, "Let's say, unless I had to."

"So why did you have to, now?"

He looked at me without replying for a moment, and then, before he could speak again, a great shadow loomed up over us, and there was a man, young but with graying hair, holding out his hand and saying, "Bahr?"

12

BEGGARS WITH CLASS

When they reopened the district it was immediately evident that they had succeeded. Restored to how it once had been, and better: a slice of Europe; a glistening slice whose pristine beauty drew in high-end stores, their high-end prices filtering out the déclassé shoppers who had filled the streets through the period of its decline.

Seeing the district restored to its former glory, one of the project's wealthy backers felt tears come to his eyes. He lived in a private residence to which he shipped the most beautiful, rarest, and largest flowers in the world. Being a man in his fifties, he had never witnessed this former glory for himself, but in his mind's eye he held an image of how it must have been, and it filled him with pride to see it made real.

One official, a recent appointee newly returned with private medical team in tow from a life and career in Berlin, noticed something nobody else had considered, something that left the district, for all its Europeanness, somehow un-European. In a flash of inspiration, he put his finger on the problem: the squares and street corners lacked the one thing that marks public spaces in Europe. Street performers! Buskers! Musicians and magicians, singers and artists, filling the streets with merriment while at their side—next to their instruments or drawing materials—elegant berets lay unobtrusively inverted so that the passers-by could give *what* they wanted, *if* they wanted—not harassed or bullied, but from a natural generosity rendered even more pliant and tender by the performance.

Beggars in Egypt, even traditional favorites like fire-eaters, had let their skills degrade and go into decline. The entry of large numbers of newcomers into the trade, that didn't help. But then, as economic circumstances declined still further, they were joined on the streets by half the population and the profession was no longer a profession. As even the desire to pretend faded, as the effort required to fake the look of a traditional beggar became too much, the old schools and guilds died off. A beggar no longer shammed wiping the windshield of your car or claimed he wanted to sell you some tissues. Feigned injuries were out, and female beggars wouldn't thrust babes-in-arms at you while crying that they were ill or dying, or whatever. Where were the people swearing to have lost their wallets and asking the fare of a train ticket back to their village? No more dramatics. Now, a beggar simply sidled up to you, or just waited for you to sidle up to them, and then, dressed pretty much the same as you, just... asked for money. In the same tone you might ask the time.

This had its upside. People were free to refuse with the same casual spontaneity and feel no guilt.

Occasionally, despite the police's best efforts to drive them off or disappear them (when they weren't already undetectable in the uniform of the average citizen), a few beggars would still manage to sneak onto the renovated streets of this Little Occident. But of course, they were not what was wanted *at all*.

The desire for perfection gave birth to an unconventional strategy. Secret orders were issued: start to recruit from the ranks of the jobless, from graduates of the music academies and art schools, and persuade them down to the district. Some had to be seduced; others could be asked outright. As their numbers climbed, officials devised a set of covert tests to filter for the finest ones and assign them plots at the choicest squares and intersections, where they could display their craft and skill to best advantage for the benefit of tourists, shoppers, and residents. For the privilege, they had to purchase a day pass like those distributed to car guards or anyone else who worked in the district's streets.

It wasn't just their gifts that impressed pedestrians. These beggars had good manners, too. They had breeding. Most were graduates, albeit from distant rural districts, since locals couldn't risk the indignity of running into friends or acquaintances and the spread of gossip.

One day, a particularly talented violinist stepped forward to buy his pass. The official behind the counter glanced at the violinist's permit then demanded to see his official ID. He glanced at the ID, then peered at the ID, then looked hard at the violinist's face and said, "Whose picture is this?"

At which the musician, surrounded by his fellow beggars with their instruments and sketchpads and costumes, said, "Mine."

Again, the official peered at the ID, then held it up to show the two men who were standing in line behind the violinist. The first lowered the saxophone in his hand, took a close look, and shrugged. The second slipped his juggling balls back in his bag, leaned forward, and examined first the photograph, then the violinist's face.

"To be honest, it looks nothing like you."

Rage supplanted surprise in the violinist's soul. He looked around but no one there knew him. The fact was, he'd always been slightly embarrassed at having to keep company with these so-called colleagues and had showed little inclination to make friends. An attitude whose price he paid, because now they all forsook him.

The official handed his card back: "Get a new ID, and don't come back till it's got a picture that looks like you."

13

BEWARE FLOWERS

Alya's miracles didn't stop at the universe of sounds in her throat.

We were at the movie theater this one time; the auditorium was crammed. We were in our seats, we'd only been there a few minutes, when she said, "I'm cold, really cold," and hunched her shoulders. It was confusing—I felt fine, and so, it seemed, did everyone else—but I put my arm around her all the same. Then, minutes into the film, I started to feel an icy trickle down the middle of my back, which quickly spread through my body. I immediately understood that it was the air conditioners: set at full power to counteract the crowd, they were now defeating us.

Or maybe, I thought, it was the power of suggestion, transmitted from Alya's body to mine.

Fresh proof of her talents came daily.

Alya stared out of the window at the autumn sky,

then turned to me, face shining, and asked, "Think it'll rain?" More an expression of joy than a question. She was looking at me with a strange yearning, as though I were the one who would bring the rain.

I shrugged. "Who knows?"

But as soon as we'd sat to eat we heard drops patter on the pane. At first, it was as though we were hearing things, but then it gathered into a steady drumming, and Alya turned in her chair to look out at the sky. She seemed lost in her happiness. I stared at her, amazed. Her tongue was clicking and popping, singing the sound of the rain, and as she ate she swayed her head to left and right, to a rhythm only she could hear.

Another time, that same extraordinary winter, she told me that when she arrived from the country where she'd been raised, she was struck by how little it rained here. She had started watching out for it, as alert to the signs of it as the small creatures snug in their burrows or sheltering in the trees' canopy. And she had learned its names. Her voice firm and clear, she said, "That thundering is *hazim*. The raindrops pounding the street outside? *Waqaa*."

Then she said, "Let's go."

We were in a café where I liked to sit. Half its complement of tables and chairs looked out over a quiet street that always seemed to enjoy its own private sense of order—the tall buildings surrounding it kept off the burning sun, while its distance from the main road held the roar of cars at bay. The presence of several government agencies nearby protected against dirt and disorder.

We had sat down. The café was half-full. I was drinking my coffee and she was drinking grape juice and humming when suddenly she said: "Let's go."

I wasn't in the habit of arguing, since once her mood was spoiled it would never be recovered by debate. She paid the bill, picked up her bag, and strode away. Before we'd even turned off the quiet street we heard a loud commotion, then the sound of something breaking. Out of nowhere, a fight had broken out in the café we'd just left. Less a daytime quarrel than a dive-bar brawl. Screams in the air and customers scattering in all directions. Without seeing who was fighting or why, Alya and I turned away and kept on walking and we never went back there again.

One night, an old tree behind my apartment toppled over, blocking the road and destroying two unlucky cars. I only saw it the next morning. I stood there, looking at the tree, and inside me was this strange contented certainty that such things would never happen to me: at least, as long as Alya was with me, I'd never be taken unawares. So I used to tell her, and she'd laugh. She would say I made it sound like magic, and I'd reply, "Well, what else could it be?"

It was like she gave no thought to her answer— the words flowed from her lips without hesitation, as though she'd always known the explanation. And what she said was that she, Alya, hadn't changed like the rest of humanity had changed after committing the crime of civilization. Her body still worked the way our ancestors' had in prehistory ("That ugly term!" she said). She sensed what everybody should be able to sense: danger, in order to avoid it; and joy, to be ready to receive it and not corrupt it.

As though to reaffirm her connection to the ancestors, she only ate fruits and vegetables. A completely plant-based existence. She seemed quite happy like that, in harmony. I pointed out that the people who'd lived in the caves and forests had never had any issue with hunting. She said, "That's the men. Savages then and since. But my foremothers were foragers. They took their fruits from nature's table."

This philosophizing on plants and the past used to make me laugh. A few minutes of conversation with Alya would leave me feeling like we were sitting in some rainforest thousands of years ago. I could almost hear the swish of gigantic butterflies, the rush of water through Amazon trees. And Alya always in her scruffy clothes, the loose men's shirts and the trousers that dropped to the floor as soon as she stepped indoors, where she would sit, silent and seductive, hair a tangle and her eyes as green as the forests in her mind. I would feel the pulse of distant drums, would sway to their beat and cry out like an animal when they fell still. I would cry out, her eyes wide-open before me, her voice away in registers where I could not follow.

But one night she woke up, and woke me. Her terrified voice in the dark, repeating:

"Something is going to happen. Something bad is going to happen."

I hardly lifted my head from the pillow, but I reached out my hand to touch her face.

"What is it, darling?"

And I waited for her to tell me her dream, the nightmare.

But she didn't. "What dream?" she said, bewildered. "I wasn't dreaming. What do dreams have to do with the future? You don't believe in that nonsense, do you?"

I smiled, "But don't you have the gift of prophecy?"

With pride, as though her words were the very pinnacle of rationality, she replied, "Not prophecy. It's a feeling, and it hasn't misled me yet."

After that, Alya never left my side. Literally. She went everywhere with me. If I got up to get a drink or go to the bathroom, she'd pad after me like a kitten. "Tied to your leg," she said, wryly, "that's what my grandmother used to say."

"Do the sound of a cat."

She frowned, "This isn't a puppet show."

And I pictured her as a puppet, dancing in a booth, enchanting the children the way she'd enchanted me.

"Won't you tell me about your dream?" I pressed her from time to time, but she gave me nothing.

"There was no dream." But laying her head in my lap, she'd lift her gaze to mine, and say, "Hold me tight. Something bad is going to happen."

My heart a handkerchief, pegged out on the line in a storm.

I pretended otherwise, but that warning of hers, that something bad was going to happen, was a constant source of terror to me. The worst thing was its vagueness; unlike her other predictions it didn't say that something was going to happen in a few minutes or a few hours, but was instead like foreboding in a dream, ill-defined but inescapable. As though her ear was tuned to fate and had picked up a voice speaking in anger but was unable to pick out the words. She couldn't understand what was being said, and she couldn't turn it into good news.

That same nebulous sense of dread filled my chest as Bahr and I surveyed the steeply rising road they called Simon Street. We didn't need to check we were in the right place: the rumors turned out to be true; children had been banned from the street.

The children kept being hit by the flowers. Plenty of injuries, quite aside from the deaths. They hit so hard, the giant blooms that Raef Annabawi had first seen on a trip to Indonesia, deciding on the spot that these were the beauties with which he'd fill his hanging garden in Muqattam.

A gigantic plant, massive, more than ten feet high—nearly twice the height of Raef himself. Rare and expensive, true, but nothing was too costly for Annabawi. Ever since he had built his extraordinary villa atop one of Muqattam's rocky outcrops and surrounded it on all sides with terraces of herbs and flowers, he had been contemplating a wall to enhance not only his garden's security and privacy, but its beauty as well. What to do? He didn't want a fence of steel or a screen of stone. Then he took that trip and found what he'd been looking for: the flower. The first time he encountered it in that Indonesian greenhouse, a young woman was standing on tiptoe, arm stretched above her head in a vain attempt to touch the bloom itself: a bright dish from whose center rose an erect blade. The sight touched off thoughts both sexual and mildly derisive in Annabawi's mind, and he drew closer. A foul reek struck him. *Titan arum!* he thought, *The corpse flower!*

Raef wasn't deterred. The look of the thing, its mythic dimensions, and the fact that it bloomed so rarely (once a decade) more than outweighed the problem of the smell. The flowers would line the outside of the wall; their stink wouldn't reach him, wouldn't even reach to the street far below. The pedestrians on Simon Street would see the impossible things looming over them like something out of sci-fi.

But the winter wind proved itself their match. A flower was toppled from its lofty perch to shatter the windshield of a car whose owner had parked there just minutes before. The driver stood, alone in the winter silence, gaping at the broken glass and the inverted plant whose upper half now occupied the two front seats. And when at last—with a herculean effort—he managed to pull it free, he got back into his damaged vehicle and started driving around and around, trying to get closer to the house on the hill. And failing. Around and around he went through the quiet paved lanes, never any closer to the looming walls,

MOHAMED KHEIR

and when, exhausted and defeated, he finally stopped, he looked down to see two thin streams of blood running from his wrist where it had been punctured by the plant's great spines. Only then did he smell it.

A few days later, a young mother locked the brake on her child's stroller and went rummaging through her handbag, searching for a ringing phone. She had found it, and was talking and laughing into the receiver, when there was a sudden crash, and she looked up to find that her little boy was gone and in his place, a colossal green body, like a distended rose upended: base over tip; stem over bloom. A flower more massive than she'd ever seen, like a prop from a sci-fi movie. Silently, apprehensively, people gathered around her, staring in disbelief as the boy's thin wail rose up between the leaves.

The first person to be killed wasn't anywhere near the villa. The wind plucked a corpse flower and bore it several streets away through the air, like a warplane, like a catastrophe looking for company. It found its victim in a five-year-old boy riding his tricycle. Just before the plant came to earth a gust caught it and sent it rocketing parallel with the road, as massive as a careening car. It smacked into the child and lifted him into the air before shredding them both, boy and bloom, against a wall.

Below the wall on which the flowers roosted, I walked with Bahr, looking for some trace of disaster but finding nothing. No shattered glass, no gore, just a too-quiet street, with hardly a pedestrian in sight and only the occasional car. No shops, no cafés, no trucks,

88

and at the top of the hill ahead, a frieze of high walls and trees. The plants above us were densely packed, but none looked especially large. Perhaps the flowers had been removed. Perhaps this was the wrong villa. Our toes were rubbed raw by the steep climb and the gravel, and I was on the point of asking Bahr, not for the first time, just where he got his information from, when suddenly he paused, peered intently at the wall beside him. He brought out his little camera, glanced briefly around at the empty street, took a picture, and set off again. I looked, but at first I couldn't see a thing. Then, along the base of the wall, I made out writing, crudely painted and almost worn away. A single phrase: Beware giant flowers.

We saw the sign and its bizarre warning, and course we didn't take it seriously. We didn't beware, and we would pay the price.

We didn't beware the day the chants came, their protest dressed in heartfelt songs that broke over the balcony and washed into the living room where we sat. Alya pricked up her ears and mewed like a cat. Then she was pulling me toward the front door as I tugged her back to the sofa.

"Come on, let's go down. Just five minutes. There's no harm in looking."

We looked down from the balcony. We couldn't see the ground through the people.

I did warn her.

"What am I, Alya? What are we? Shadows on the wall, Alya. A mirror that mirrors back but does not see, an unseen breeze. Just a breeze, demurely passing by and minding its business. Two lovers sitting together in a corner, our feet tucked in so as not to trip time in its march."

But she laughed and pulled me anyway. She cooed to me, sang me strains of desire, and made (though I couldn't say how) the sound of hope. And the songbirds, long forgotten in my breast, woke up. She pressed her ear to my chest and listened to the birds and whispered something to them, then she got to her feet. She grasped my hand and we went through the door together.

"Five minutes," she said. Just a brief excursion into the world, that was all she wanted. A group photo with progress, a selfie with the march of time. So, what was it I was doing? Why did I suddenly decide we should stay out? What was I searching for? Or perhaps I should say, what was I trying to make up for, to excuse? I ask myself that sometimes—the times I forget that I already know the answer.

Whatever. We went downstairs hand in hand, never to return together.

A couple of men, not from the city as far as I could tell, asked me for a blanket, and though I'd brought two blankets with me, I was selfish and said, "No." I wanted them, one for the earth and one for the heavens. The men nodded and went on sitting there on the bare ground, cross-legged.

We laid out on the edge of the sidewalk, next to a cluster of small tents and blankets on which some people were sleeping, while others sprawled, uncovered and awake. The stars seemed close when we looked up. The glare from a streetlight was impossible to ignore. "Just reach out and switch it off," I said. "I want to sleep."

She began to hum. She said, "Do you know the outdoor lullaby?"

"Never heard of it."

She brought her lips right up to my ear and began to murmur. I was trying to make out the words, and watching the streetlight flare beneath the starlight, I asked myself if the light was happy for us, or whether, in its loneliness, it envied us.

Alya sang. Like all the singing I'd ever known all run together in one moment, in that tune: my mother's songs, the honey-seller outside my school, the laundromat's radio carried to our ears as we turned out the lights to sleep.

I remembered something. I said, "This once you guessed wrong."

She looked at me, questioning, and I reminded her of the night she'd woken full of foreboding.

Through the rough music of the crowds she stared at me, quite silent. Then, as though we both knew the answer, she asked, "You really think I was wrong?"

14

COLD THEORY

"It came to me during a storm," said Bahr. "Back when Europe was home." He hooked his forefingers around the word "home," a bookish gesture quite out of keeping with the neighborhood through which we were walking, in search of a football field we weren't even sure still existed. But Bahr didn't care, and went on as though he were reading from a book:

It rained continuously that night, its drumming like the underpinning of an overture, and people plunged headfirst into the gathering dark with their overcoats clamped against the gale and umbrellas open. They scurried back and forth as though they were being pushed or pulled by soft hands in the wind. Despite the crackling thunder and the banging rain I felt more content than I'd been since I was in my mother's womb. This beautiful, blustery weather, I said to myself, is what built civilization here. Here, you have to work for your warmth. There's no time to idle on the corner, to loiter around. No place for wolf whistles and catcalls down a block. Pause for a single second and the skies will drown you, the cold will freeze you solid.

People in winter clothes are always more beautiful, more elegant. Dark overcoats against white snow sharpens both extremes and makes both lovelier. There's no sun to spoil the skin, no heat to squat on the chest and throttle your strength and energy and ambition. Cold here is a spur, and the pouring rains that join earth to heaven promote a perpetual verdure that the children of the desert can only picture as their paradise. Here, their heaven of green gardens and rain are as commonplace as the wind: perennial. Anything that can build with such beauty, that grows from this blessed rain: of course it turned out well.

And cold enjoins love: bodies warm each other in its embrace, kisses become hot drops for the soul. The desert, meanwhile, turns the same clinch into a hell. The heat dulls sex, turns all affection beyond mere talk and virginal flirting into a trial, and makes it hateful. Like harassment: speech or touch without the true care of the embrace. Harassment is our sex.

There hadn't been a breath of wind that whole time, so who knows what made Bahr think of the cold. But the night I spent on the street with Alya, in the streetlight and laughter, it had been freezing. We dozed on the sidewalk as content as in our bed and were woken at dawn by the zealous at their morning drills. Alya looked tired. "Come on," I said, "I'll walk you to your friend's place." The friend lived close by and when we got to her door, Alya turned to me and said, "Are you going home? I'll come with you."

I said, "No. I'm going back to the square."

And I did, going back through the intoxicated joy of the early morning streets. The crowds were already thinning, and the square seemed empty without Alya, so I told myself I would go home, go upstairs, eat, and rest for a while. I'd change my clothes and come back down.

At home I showered, ate what I could find, and first sat, then stretched out, on the sofa. When I saw that I'd left my phone unplugged, I reached out to connect it to the charger, but my groping fingers fell short and I couldn't be bothered to get up. I'll just close my eyes for a few minutes, I thought, then I'll plug it in. I shifted my head to a more comfortable position. In no time, I was gone.

It was dark when I woke, and I lurched upright in a panic. Grabbing the phone, I remembered that the battery was dead, so I pushed the charger into its socket and waited for it to turn on, then to pick up a network. There was an incredible number of missed calls. I called up the list of numbers; they were all from Alya. I stared at the screen.

I called her. Her phone was off. I scrambled into my clothes, but just before I left, I switched on the television. In mounting shock I began flipping through the channels. The violence, the blood. People being run down. People stabbing and being stabbed.

I tore downstairs like a madman, trying her number over and over again, then made straight for the building where I'd dropped her off earlier. I knocked, but no one answered.

Later, I found out that she had seen the protests on TV and, terrified, had called me. When she was unable to get through she sprinted down to the square. It was after she arrived, all alone, all alone despite the thousands around her, that it happened.

After she was gone, I kept dreaming of what happened. But different. Like, in the dream, the sky was full of fireworks and bright colors, and everyone had joined the protest, and the apartments all stood empty. The breeze was breath, was sighs and dreams, and it wasn't your legs that carried you, but the surge of packed bodies. The joy you could see in their eyes. As if everyone could forgive everyone. And there, amid those millions, I challenged Alya: "Come, can you sing something greater than this?"

But she just smiled. There were tears in her eyes, she was saying something I couldn't hear, and I pulled her to me with my right arm, while with my left I cleared a path through the throng. Though we were all one body, so we didn't feel the jostle and stumble of flesh, the rub of clothes. I was pulling Alya gently by the hand so she wouldn't slip away, but then something was wrong, something unfamiliar in her touch against my palm, and looking behind me I saw that I was holding the hand of another woman, who was staring back at me with an expression somewhere between astonishment and disgust. I stammered an apology and looked past her, where I could see Alya as she fell further and further behind, her lips wide as though she were screaming. I tried pushing back to her against the flow of bodies, the joyous roaring river, but couldn't.

PART TWO

_____

ALMOST FOREVER

1

HIS COMMANDS

Ahmed woke with a start. His father was gone from the bedroom door. He went into the living room, still trembling at hearing the warm timbre of his father's voice. It rang in his ears as he came to the door of his mother's room, then pushed and entered.

A rattling groan swelled over the dawn prayers from the Sidi El Ghobashy mosque. He lurched forward in alarm. "Mother!" Shaking her, weeping. "Mother!"

She wasn't quite gone, though, and he managed to bring her back from the brink—looking twenty years older, but alive. Moving and speaking, still transmitting instructions from a father, who—after that one visit—had seemingly broken off all contact with his son.

The story of his father's intervention and the last-minute rescue spread among relatives, then neighbors. They began to question the mother—shyly at first and then insistently—about her visions of the departed and what he said.

And his mother picked up where she had left off: a conduit for each installment of advice, for whose sagacity and sound sense the only equal was the next. Ahmed, meanwhile, returned to his suspicions. And yet... And yet, he'd never known his mother to speak this way before. This was his father's wisdom. His father's strength and cruelty, too.

And the more people speculated and asked questions, the more they sought to benefit from her visions, her prudent revelations, the more his mother withdrew.

"Your father isn't dead," she would say, strength coursing through the words that pushed their way out through the lines and wrinkles around her mouth, old age fogging the femininity of her voice until it sometimes seemed to actually *be* his father's. He would watch her as she sat alone, muttering and waving her hands as if talking to someone, but he never had the courage to approach her.

It was now common knowledge that, despite his death, his father was still alive. Relatives and neighbors in search of guidance gathered daily outside the family home. One day, Ahmed dozed off on the sofa for a few minutes, and he saw his father again. This time, he didn't speak. He was carrying an old brown suitcase with a broken handle, and he opened the front door of the apartment as if to leave. Then he paused in the doorway and called out, "Bye then, Sayyida."

Ahmed glanced at the door to his mother's bedroom and sensed movement, footsteps approaching. He woke and heaved himself to his feet. There was no sound as he entered the room. He stood by the door looking down at her body, so still and silent it might have been lying there for a thousand years. Though he was quite sure, he reached out a hand and shook her anyway. The body rocked in answer, then stilled, and he smelled death. He wondered what he would say to the crowd outside who had all come for guidance.

2

THEY DIDN'T SEEM SAD; JUST NOT ENTIRELY PRESENT, PERHAPS

It began a couple of weeks after I lost Alya.

The first dead person I saw was Hassan Yaqout, sitting alone at the Tawfiq Café as was his habit, and smoking a narghile. We used to call the place The One Man Café because it was so small; we couldn't understand how it managed to stay open with just two tables for its customers.

The past few years had been so eventful that I'd quite forgotten Hassan Yaqout was dead. It had been a car accident, three or four years ago. A Peugeot taxi with its complement of seven passengers had overturned on the way back from his home district in Beni Sueif, where they made the little rugs and earrings that he hawked to tourists and students in the city.

I wasn't thinking of the accident when I saw Hassan. I wasn't thinking about him at all. My gaze passed over him quite by chance and took him in, sitting there as I'd seen him hundreds of times before.

I kept driving, but after I'd negotiated the car through the traffic of Maarouf Street, just as I turned right onto Talaat Harb, it struck me that he was dead. I stopped my little '92 Suzuki dead in the middle of the road, deaf to the horns and obscenities that sounded in protest.

I waited until my heart slowed, then I made another right, taking Mahmoud Basyouni to Ramses, then back onto Maarouf, and there he was again, still sitting in the café. But as I came closer, full of foreboding, I saw that it was someone else. A man whose build and posture were very similar to Hassan's, but even so, was someone else entirely. The air rushed back through my lungs and I rolled past him, fingers trembling on the wheel.

Next was Amany Assayyid, the delicate and self-effacing poet who, in the isolation of her solitary existence, had been overrun and killed by cancer many months before I watched her riding the escalator down into the hordes of the Ramses metro station as I rode up on the escalator alongside.

In the simple blue dress she always wore, she slid past me in the grip of the crowd. Demure, with the same distracted air she'd had in life. Involuntarily, I halted my slow plod upward, my neck pulling my head around to follow her, but the rush hour crowds pressed me on and I nearly tripped as I crested the escalator. This time I couldn't retrace my steps to check on whom, or what, I'd seen.

This confusion over faces—I use the term confusion because it shields me from more frightening possibilities—began to occur more and more frequently. Two days after I caught sight of Amany, old Zeinhom peeped out from the entrance of the neighborhood grocery store, as if watching over things until his son got back from mosque, then ducked back inside. I was too scared to step into the shop's dim interior to check. I'd been forced to attend Zeinhom's wake a few months earlier: the chairs put out for the event had blocked the entrance to our building.

In most cases, though, the dead appeared at a distance—in a vehicle if I was on foot, walking if I was driving—and often with a distracted air, as though still preoccupied with life's problems. When I say confusion... It was like the day I walked into my humble provincial university for the first time, and found myself confronted with thousands of new faces. I kept imagining I'd seen someone I knew, but every time the similarity would prove to be an illusion, masking a stranger.

Faces in faces, that's what it was. People taking shape in others: friends in strangers, the dead in the living. When I was able to catch up with them, they were always revealed to be some other person altogether. But who knows, maybe that other person was also dead, gazing out through the eyes of yet another.

Deepening my confusion, the dead people I saw had nothing in common. I was just as likely to see someone who had passed away when I was a child as someone who'd died just days or weeks earlier. I saw a fellow conscript from the army (training accident), and I saw an old lady who'd been my grandmother's neighbor back when Grandma had still been alive herself (anaphylactic shock, courtesy of an allergy to cats); and in the line at the Giza Zoo I even saw my cousin's son, who'd been carried off by a fever at the age of three. He was standing there, happily clasping the hand of Miss Sanaa, my primary school teacher. I'd heard no news of Miss Sanaa since I'd been in her class. Had she died too? I wondered. Had death brought her here?

When I met him two years or more after these sightings began, Bahr would persuade me that I should start from the premise that there must be a connection. I mustn't be complacent, he would say; I mustn't accept the idea of coincidence. But at the time I couldn't see any connection between the things I saw. Or maybe I could *see* it but couldn't *recognize* it. Or, if I was able to recognize it, however vaguely, then I was simply unable to explain.

Alya went away and left me seeing the dead. Simply at first—if that's the expression I want—just walking by, or riding escalators, or jammed in crowds. Then I started to see them up close, in more complex, intimate scenes: talking or laughing and always in the company of the dead like them.

3

_____

HIS AUDIENCE

Which of them owned the other? Him or Sherine? He had learned her name the day she first asked him to sing. Enchanted by her, a sudden surge of courage had made him take a chance, and the next thing he knew he was listening in astonishment to the effortless flow of his voice. Was it the booze? Was it her?

The first hypothesis foundered when she asked him to sing in front of her friends. He'd downed drink after drink and it hadn't helped at all. But later that same night he sang to her on the restaurant's veranda and the nightingale returned to his throat.

Time and again it was confirmed: the only company in which his stutter disappeared was hers. She was his only audience, and he was her songbird, creating and performing for her and her alone; composing only what he thought would please his audience of one. Sherine Alalayli.

It was almost enough for him. Then she invited him to her home.

His heart shook, resisting hope.

Warily: "You're having a party?"

With an expression he couldn't read at all, she answered, "Since when do you sing at parties?"

Then she gave him a wink and his heart danced.

The tongue is the gateway to the world, and the world is a woman. How to cross that threshold without stumbling? The sentries would see through him as soon as the first two syllables were out, before he'd even managed to utter his name.

But there he was at the appointed time, standing dumbstruck before the fantastically proportioned building. It seemed to reach the sky. About to step inside, he hesitated, remembering that he had to show his ID to the guard. The guard glanced at it and let him pass.

The thirty-second floor.

Lost in the palatial elevator. His first thought as he'd stepped inside was that it must be the lobby. He declined to sit on a vast sofa and gave the fully uniformed attendant the floor number. The attendant pushed the button without acknowledging he'd heard.

That's the floor, but what's the apartment number? He kept the thought to himself, and when the lift stopped and the doors opened, he realized how foolish he'd been: a hallway lined with clipped shrubbery and a single lofty doorway at the far end. He approached the door and had raised his hand to knock when it opened. A beautiful Asian woman looked out from behind the door.

Still tucked behind the door, the maid gestured for him to step inside. He did so, and was immediately swallowed by sheer space; he felt as if he were foundering in the carpet. The maid went ahead and he followed. He had imagined that they would be going to the living room but was led instead into a maze of corridors. He knew they must be corridors, because they were inside an apartment after all, but he'd known alleyways, streets in fact, that had been narrower.

They came at last to a door. A bedroom door, to his surprise. The room was vast, and Sherine was sitting up in bed, smiling and calling to him.

"Over here, Salaam!"

The maid withdrew, and he stood there, awestruck.

Was this how it was going to be?

It suddenly occurred to him just how little experience he had, and he told himself that he would fail, and felt afraid. Only when Sherine called his name a second time did he realize that he'd been drifting.

Tentatively he approached the bed.

Was that surprise on Sherine's face? She was wearing a shirt and very short shorts, and when eventually he reached her she gestured to the sofa by the bed and said, "Sit." He tottered to the sofa and sat down, all at sea and soaked in sweat.

As she gazed at him (from eyes which in that moment were the most important things in his life) he was possessed by that particular spirit which overtakes men when their manhood is put to the test. Capable of anything and no clue where to begin. But there she was, resting on her side facing him. She smiled and said, "Sing, Salaam."

For a moment he froze, then swallowed and started to sing. He botched the first line and panic seized him, but his voice quickly leveled out. Not loud, not soft, but pitched somewhere in between, he sang as she gazed at him and smiled. Then she turned onto her other side and he was singing to her back. The neat buttocks filling the little shorts. For a brief moment he fell silent, at a loss, but she spoke again, "Go on, Salaam," so on he went, watching as she tugged the sheet up to her waist, the backside vanishing beneath it, but still present, like a promise. He sang, his heart pouring like smoke from his mouth, until he had to break off to take a drink from the glass of water next to him. As he opened his mouth to sing again, he caught the sound of her breathing, calm and even.

Softly, he called her name, then a little louder, but she had drifted away. He got to his feet at the very moment the maid reappeared and beckoned to him. Time to leave.

He followed her back down the same corridors, and this time it seemed that he could hear sounds and voices floating from the doorways as they passed. The maid brought him to the front door, opened it, and asked him to wait for a moment. She produced an envelope from her pocket and held it out. He took it instinctively, without a second thought, and then it struck him. He gaped at her, but she met his surprise with a professional smile and motioned to the door.

Only when he was back home did he pluck up the courage to open it. He closed his front door, peeled back the flap, and gasped audibly at the quantity and denomination of the bills that lay within.

It wasn't in him to take offense. When the next invitation came, he went. She told him, "The first time I heard your voice it threw me into an extraordinary state of calm, as though nothing in the world mattered. You're the one, Salaam, I told myself. You're the cure to my insomnia.

"Anyway, how much do you make at the moment?"

He tried balancing his schedule. Mornings at the office, her apartment at night, occasional daytime excursions, the long lonely walks that kept him company like a friend. In fact, his desire to balance his two worlds was not financially motivated—Sherine gave him his office salary many times over—it was because he didn't want her to possess him completely. His inability to sing in front of anyone else didn't leave him with many options. Just as a man can't be his own judge and jury, no artist can work with an audience of one. This peculiar situation was, he sensed, the world's final and most inexcusable insult. Yet he also knew that he would never find the strength to walk away from the intimacy offered him by a woman who hadn't ever come to visit him, not even in his dreams.

His dreams, with their endless, monotone variations on melancholy. Recently, though, a new one had been added to the roster:

He was sitting in a reception room. It was unfamiliar to him, yet he knew that it was somewhere in Sherine's apartment. There was this tiny cat, soft and black, twisting over and around him on the sofa where he sat. He'd push the cat away, but it would climb back up, stalking along the backrest behind him, or pouncing on his bare feet, scratching them. The maid would come and take the cat away, but in no time there it would be again: the cat's hiss at his ear, its claws at his neck, and in the hiss, the sound of his favorite song on an endless loop.

4

THE SILENT TEAM

– OR –

A COG IN THE MACHINE

They had no regular schedule. They would come at any time, ball in hand, and sit in a line at the edge of the field—a dirt plot yet to host a building—following the game being played without a single cheer or comment. Then, when it was over, they would rise as one man and drift over the sidelines to face the winners.

The system was that the winning team stayed on and got to say who'd they'd play next, unless—which was more often the case with the silent team—there was no one waiting to play. And when no one was waiting, and when they'd beaten the previous winners—and this team always beat the previous winners—they would split into two smaller teams and play each other for an hour or so before going home.

What was unusual about that team, the thing that set them apart, was that no one ever heard them say anything. They never made a sound. Not before the match, not afterward, not even (stranger still) during. They glided around the field, on the ball and off it, as if they knew their positions blindfolded, slipping preemptively into place like seers. If one of them wanted the ball passed his way, he only had to raise a hand. If a goal was scored, the scorer would jog a couple of paces with his fist in the air before falling into his teammates' wordless embrace.

How did they call for a foul? The player would stop running, then the rest would follow his lead, standing as still as statues, each man pointing to the spot. And if anyone called for a foul against them, they would either accede to the request (wordlessly again) or shake their heads and play on, and their opponents were never brave enough to object.

One day, though, an opponent *did* object. After the foul was given, the silent team stopped playing altogether: they took their ball and started to walk off. The opponent objected to this as well, and grabbed a member of the silent team by his shirt. Pulled hard. But the roles were rapidly reversed, and the objecting player found himself being hit harder than he'd ever been hit in his life.

Screaming, blood pouring from his nose, the victim dropped to the ground, while his team began to form a circle around their silent counterparts. They didn't dare to return the blow, though, just squared up, shouting, and this shouting grew in both volume and intensity until it had turned to insults. The vilest obscenities. But not a word in reply. The silent team stood there, staring at their abusers—and not a word.

Gradually, the victim's team fell silent too, and went to help their teammate off the ground. At which point the oldest player on the silent team approached the injured man, put a hand on his shoulder, and spoke. One word:

"Sorry."

First, the depth of the voice, and the incongruities in the accent, and only then were we alerted to the fact that the darkness of their faces was not quite the same as our lighter darkness, and, suddenly, we *saw*. Their leader spoke this single word of apology in his strange accent and then, before our wondering gaze, turned back to his players and motioned them on with both his hands. A ripple passed through them, then they all moved as one off the field, calmly and quietly, a single wave soon to break and disperse to their homes in distant districts of the city.

It was the last time we saw them. Who knows how many times we played football in the years that followed, expecting them to show again? We arranged matches and put on tournaments, winning or losing but never, not one of us, free of the feeling that the true victory was the one we'd never achieved.

The story didn't end there. Bahr and I were standing in a souq for second-hand appliances and junk when Bahr suddenly picked up where he had left off. This market had once been where they played, he explained. The football field. He said:

Years later, I saw the captain again. It was in that northern country, at some event for refugees from all over the world. He was chatting in the Eritrean booth. Hesitantly, I approached and introduced myself, realizing as I did so that I knew absolutely nothing about him, not even his name. He looked at me with a slight air of bewilderment, returned my greeting, then turned back to resume his conversation. It was the same voice which had apologized that night, long ago. I hung around for a moment or two, unable to think of anything more to say, and when at last he glanced back at me inquiringly, I lowered my head and left. At that point in my life I was living the way he'd always lived: in flight from one place to another. There was always a bag—slightly bigger than this one—standing ready by my door.

Bahr gave his satchel a shake.

It contained my most important possessions. I kept it there so I'd be ready to leave at a moment's notice, the moment life laid down the law: a raid by immigration, or by another group of immigrants; the landlord come knocking to collect his rent; an invitation from a friend to come and stay somewhere else, which might be no better than another vile room in an even viler neighborhood.

It was a few days after the officer's shoe pressed me into the dirt of the prison yard that I packed the bag for the first time. They'd taken us back inside to the filth and vermin of the cells. This time, I didn't hear or see Soha or any other women. We were there for a day or two, maybe more, before they let some of us go, including me. As they escorted us outside, there were tables by the gate with young officers sitting at them, laughing. Some prisoners were making complaints. A few were still in handcuffs. One was tugging the waistband of his pants up as blood ran down from his stomach, but he was talking to the officer as though nothing was the matter.

They sat us on the ground beside a man who was making tea and coffee for the officers and conscripts. There was this air of business-as-usual to everything going on around us. The handcuffs were biting into the man I was cuffed to. He was moaning and it was grating on my nerves. I was too thin for the cuffs to hurt me. Nearby, there was a woman in a black robe clutching a plastic suitcase and talking with a little girl of about twelve. From time to time they would turn to look at us, then go back to talking. I assumed at first that they must be talking about us, but after a while I realized what it was: They were looking at us the way you might look at a chair, say, at any inanimate object that might happen to fall in your line of sight. We were nothing. Or rather, we were just part of the scenery, and would be even if we were to start bleeding out altogether, like the man hitching at his pants.

Then I saw my parents. My father was talking to a conscript by the gate, wearing an expression I'd never seen on him or anyone else before: an extraordinary blend of weariness, rage, worry, and humiliation, and I wished I could shrink where I sat, grow smaller and smaller until I disappeared into one of the tiny holes the ants had opened in the walls. Then, all of a sudden, there was my mother, kissing the conscript's hand.

Their voices didn't reach me where I sat. I watched the scene play out silently:

My mother's body, rarely seen outside our house, stooped in the reeking yard to kiss the hand of a young conscript who could do nothing in any case, not for her and not for me. My mother, abasing herself without realizing that she had no hope of getting anything in return. I watched my father step back and stare at her. His back was turned to me, but I could picture the shock on his face.

It was in that moment that I understood, Seif: If you rebel against fate, if you insist on being master of what you call Your Destiny (the insolence!), then life itself might come out and force your mother to her knees.

That day, life chose to let me go, though my release had nothing to do with my mother's kiss. They left us in the yard past noon, then undid our cuffs and made us sign papers, and we were allowed to leave. As I signed my name to testimony I had never spoken, the officer said with a smile that we'd meet again soon.

Since that day, I've made a habit of keeping that little bag packed. When I still lived at home, I kept it under the bed, a secret from my mother. It stood by the front door after I moved. You would know my home—or to be precise, the place where I was staying—by a small bag packed and ready by the door.

Not just a change of clothes or two, but books as well, mostly collections of short stories plus digests and essays. Big books, the long novels, were beyond me; I had the powerful and unshakable conviction that the house would be raided before I'd gotten a quarter of the way through, before I'd be done with the introduction. Unshakable, I say, and furthermore, one that expanded to all areas of my life. I came to prefer contract work, for instance, getting paid per job, and refused any regularity in my income or my hours. My whole existence revolved around a single imperative, and to disregard it would leave me struggling to breathe: I must be able to go away at any time without feeling that I was leaving a thing behind— work, possessions, people, not even unread pages in a book.

Learning to cook was out, for instance. I had no time, though I had all the time in the world. Inside me, that other clock was ticking, a constant warning against attachments. I never ate main courses but subsisted on appetizers. Like my life, I often thought: an assemblage of side plates but never the big dish; a little money, a little love, a morsel of success, but nothing that ever defined me.

That said, the first time I was ever happy with a job was at a seaside restaurant in the far north. They say the kitchen's the hardest work there is, but I was happy. For hours I did nothing but stand at the sink and wash dishes. Wash wash wash, dishes without end, as though they had the whole world dining there. Nobody ever asked more of me than to keep on going. Nobody expected me to be imaginative or inventive or to "make a suggestion." Nothing asked of me and nothing given, either—and it was part-time too. Five seconds after I was done for the night, I'd be in the street and free as a bird until the following afternoon. I was a cog in a machine, and how happy I was. Just a working part: no responsibility for the past, no need to worry about the future. Guiltless, conscienceless, un-responsible.

Responsibility. An odd feeling, Seif. Let me tell you how I began to understand—only hazily at first—the algorithms that run this world of ours. A while after I was released, I read an article in a medical journal about the importance of facing your fears, so I decided to go back to the yard where I had suffered that jolt of terror. Since the day I'd gotten out, just the sight of the street where the entrance to the station's yard lay would push the sweat out onto my forehead and down my neck, and throw my heartbeat into a madness. There she was again, my mother, stooped to kiss the no-name conscript's hand while my father turned that murderous, murdered look her way. I resolved to return and claim that I'd lost some documents, that I wanted to report them missing and apply for replacements.

I went up to the gate as though to the Pit of Hell itself, citizens and hawkers crowding around, while on the sidewalk men at small tables sold official stamps. The sun was strong and the stench penetrating, and I was amazed that these were the walls behind which I had felt that cold fear. I drew closer. At the gate the guard called me over (my heart nearly hopped out of my ear) and asked what I wanted. "To file a report for missing documents," I said. He reached out and rifled through my pockets, insolent and indifferent, then waved me through.

I stood in line, my heart growing calmer as I waited. The corner where I'd been sitting when I saw my parents was empty. A young desk sergeant opened a report for me, and once I'd signed he took the pen and set it down on the desk beside him. I stood there. "What are you waiting for?" he asked.

"You've got my pen."

"This is my pen," he said, disgusted.

I found myself smiling. "Well then, you keep it."

"You think you're doing me a favor?" he snapped, glaring at me. "It's mine!"

Still smiling, I left the station as calm and measured and confident as a man who came there every day, and as I passed through the gate I pushed my hand in my pocket and felt my pen. How unfair I'd been. That poor sergeant. I started to laugh. It occurred to me to call my father, to see how he was and tell him what had happened, so I went to a store across the street from the station and dialed his apartment from the phone they kept behind the counter. I called once, then again, but no one answered. Worried, I kept trying until my sister finally answered, her voice somewhere between a scream and tears.

"Baba's dead, Bahr!"

And that, Seif—though I couldn't tell at the time—was some kind of a beginning. Later, I would see that it had given me a path through life, but all I had then was how strange and indefinable it was, my father dying on the very day I'd faced down that wretched memory in which he'd figured. Like it was a punishment, say, or the price for confronting my fears, or that, having managed to actually gain one thing, I had to lose another. Or that both were aspects of the same mysterious whole; that it had to be depleted there to reach completion here.

There are laws that run beneath the surface of events without our noticing them. They only break cover and trip us when we refuse to accept our roles as cogs in the machine—when we decide to swim against the current or confront our fears as I'd done that day. That said, some aspect of these laws— these mechanisms of give and take—still manage to make their way through to us, distorted as though seen through water, garbled like prophecies. Like the heretical notion that we're each granted exactly twenty-four carats of good fortune, no more and no less, which is parceled out between health and wealth, intelligence and heredity, beauty and luck—between all those things a person hopes will be theirs. It doesn't take much experience, or a rich long life, to realize that nothing could be more misleading. I've seen women with beauty *and* brains *and* breeding *and* happiness, and others who are ugly and sick and poor, begging for bread and circling saints' tombs in the hope it will bring them children. I've seen the disfigured, missing limbs and eating from the garbage, and known mass murderers who died in their beds, a smile upon their lips because they knew there was nothing to come, no punishment and no reward. If there truly is a divine hand then it is not so much steering our course as clutching fistfuls of sand and casting them into the wind to fall as they may. That motion we call our will is just the force of the wind driving upon us: grains of sand whipped through the air.

People who don't understand this will tell you to stand firm, to fight and test yourself. "Settle down," they'll tell you, "build, accumulate." These things are chains. They'll hold you fast until fate—let's call it fate for now—until fate finally finds you, just where it wants you, and deals its blow. Has its revenge for your temerity: your conviction that you could endure. You, with your castle of sand.

I settled down myself, and it cost me Irene and Adam, my lover and my son. A single moment of foolishness. Don't stand your ground defiantly. Stay light. Flee if you can. Run before anyone entangles you. Life won't forgive you for staying crouched in a corner. That is, until everything crumbles around you. Only then might your corner save you.

In Asia, I once went to visit a very poor village in a region within the earthquake belt. They were so frequent that the people there were used to them, even slept through them. Without the money to build houses that could withstand the tremors, they built their homes without roofs. Exposed to the birds above; naked before heaven. But they still worried about the walls coming down, so they crammed everything they owned into the corners: beds, sofas, appliances (if there were any), their food. Their whole lives in the corner. Shadowed. They would wake in the morning to see the rubble in the middle of the room, the cracked stones in the courtyard; would peer out at it all from their corners, then go back to sleep.

5

ALMOST FOREVER

The road that leads abroad is better than the road around your block; the long road is better than the short. Truck over taxi, streetcar over truck, subway over streetcar, train over the lot. Train over plane, too, since the trip lasts longer.

The winding road is better than the straight one, for the same reason. Your role, Yehyia, is to take the straight road and loop it around itself, stretch it out. Your job is to obstruct the ambler, to stretch his stroll out; to ensure that the ships don't dock and the planes don't land and the traveler never arrives; to keep the road rolling on forever. And if that's too much to ask, then almost forever.

Yehyia noted that his manager was asking him for the very same files he'd requested two days before, files the manager had previously asked Yehyia to send to another department—a department that had returned them promptly and practically unchanged: a few signatures here and there; a rubber-stamp or two. The manager added his own signature and off they went again. The files consisted of personal and professional documentation belonging to the people whose bleached, passport-sized portraits were dotted throughout: notarized requests, pleas, complaints, and quotidian legal measures—a license renewal, an application for ID, inquiries about an inheritance. The files themselves circled around and around, came and went in a loop whose chronic recurrence he occasionally caught wind of when a face or name stirred a memory, though the faces and names were so alike that frequently he doubted himself. Then one day a file came back with a name he definitely hadn't forgotten—Ashgar Tawfiq, "Trees" Tawfiq—because the first time he'd seen it he had grinned to think of the woman's father gazing fondly at his garden.

So Ashgar's file came back. There was scarcely a change worth mentioning in the documents themselves or in the progress of her pension application, but this time Yehyia took a closer interest, and one day he managed to intercept Ashgar's file following yet another visit to the manager. He leafed through it, but found nothing of note. Just a new signature over a minor correction and the phrase "Forward to…" followed by the name of the department from which the file had been sent.

The days went by and Yehyia grew convinced that they, despite the hush and grandeur of his department, were doing absolutely nothing at all.

But he was wrong.

Shortly before Yehyia joined the department—or perhaps just after, but in any case before he noticed the endless looping of the files—a confidential report was issued stating that there was a surplus of dead time: a result of economic stagnation and the increase in the cost of luxuries (such as sitting around in cafés, for instance). The report calculated this surplus as an average of two hours per day per citizen. Two whole hours in which the citizen wasn't working, commuting, watching football, having sex, eating, or drinking. The hours in any given case might have varied—depending on the citizen's personal circumstances, their age, their social class—but the average was exactly two, and tallied up, those two hours meant a full day every twelve—say, three days per month, or thirty-odd days in a year. Now multiply those figures by the number of adults in Egypt (more than sixty million) and you found yourself with one billion, eight hundred million totally dead days per year. Official knees gave way at the mere thought of what could be done with this vast accumulation of days, how they might be put to use by agitators or hostile agencies or provocateurs. Swiftly and in secret, dozens of additional reports were churned out in an effort to close the breach. The best—the most natural—solution to counter their new enemy was bureaucracy. With a secrecy even more stringent and without establishing any new agencies that might draw unwanted attention, a number of individuals were recruited from existing departments and given instructions on how to occupy—that is, waste—the greatest possible amount of citizens' time, thereby sealing the rift in their days and preempting the incursion of whatever, or whoever, might lie on the other side of it.

The directives they sent out were to be implemented at the countless desks and counters of government institutions, and took the form of requests for additional documents, official stamps, countersignatures, and rare paper stamps that were only obtainable from minor functionaries who seemed to have vanished from the earth or from managers who were missing from their desks for half of every day. There were unfulfillable orders to cancel certain papers, miles of speed bumps laid down along main roads and highways, the traffic light network was reengineered to fail. Projects to build commercial centers and off-ramps and switchbacks were begun at great expense, then quietly dropped. There were rigorously executed operations to damage the pipes that carried water and sewage, to disrupt the internet, to design new and circuitous routes for public buses, to double the number of metro stations on each line—to quadruple them. Every piece—each seemingly arbitrary and unrelated to the others—was part of a vast, directed effort to cut the amount of dead time to under two hundred million days per year. But that astonishing reduction, a decrease of over ninety percent, wasn't enough. For the first time, members of parliament began replacing their traditional calls for more fines and harsher penalties and new crimes with proposals for public works projects. Traffic police and transport inspectors

and environmental investigators reported ever growing numbers of people for infringements, and the
offenders were obliged to spend hours and hours
engaged in these projects, hours that led directly to
the laying of more (twisting and roundabout) public
roads and compulsory checkpoints and toll booths,
none of which wasted more than a few minutes here
and there when taken in isolation, but which taken
together amounted to an enormous reduction in the
overall average.

Yehyia, as he later discovered, was one of the
bureaucrats tasked with carrying out this mission;
though he, like most of his fellow foot soldiers,
had no idea there was a war being fought. Only the
higher-ups, people like his boss, had the haziest sense
that something was going on, and even then most of
them assumed it was a campaign to tighten up proce-
dures and restore diligence to their ranks.

The only people who truly understood were
outside their ranks: people who'd caught wind of
something through a betrayed confidence, or the
indiscretion of a pen pusher, or even just a hunch,
subsequently confirmed by personal observation of
changes in procedure, of the many alterations to the
standards and regulations.

In the end, however rough and indistinct their
understanding of its mechanisms, the true nature of
the campaign became clear to these few. It was de-
signed to exhaust them, they now realized, to stran-
gle at birth those thoughts and dreams that need free
time to in which to take root and grow. And over

the course of numerous discussions—the duration of which were curtailed by the efficiency of the campaign in question—they came up with a solution: timeshare.

The resistance was established as a vast web without a center. Haphazardly, it grew and sprawled, man to man, man to woman, woman to woman, woman to man, and all working to the same end: that daily tasks, especially urgent ones, be shared. Going to the store to buy the staples, say, or fact-checking a work proposal, or escorting an elderly relative home. Apps tracked your progress; each time you did something for someone else, you got more…time. And at the heart of the approach was the fact that the statistics worked with averages. One person might have three free hours, another only thirty minutes, and out of this disparity came the idea of sharing time and tasks, of turning tasks into credit. Modest fortunes were made, decoupled from money and tied to time—but given the mundane nature of the tasks at hand, "modest" was as far as it went.

The concept of credit wasn't as simple as free time gained in exchange for hours of work. It meant something different for everyone. There were those who had a great deal of time left; others knew their clock was running out. Think of how many people have realized, as their life draws to an end, that the joys of life, the things they'd always longed for, will never be theirs? Then think of all the young people whose otherwise joyful lives are marred by the inescapable monotony of their workdays. Now fathers, uncles, and old men could come and drink from the young man's cup; could sample joys whose costs the young man could bear but lacked the time to enjoy. And with their hard-won experience, they could take on the tasks that youth finds so tedious, drawing up dull reports and running numbers and spreadsheeting schedules, shortening the span of a working life so a younger generation might retire at least a little earlier than their parents. Experience is a comb that life gives you only after your hair's dropped out, as the wretched proverb has it. Well, no longer. The grandmother, all alone, watching the clock and dying of boredom: so much time to kill with so many children in need of care and tenderness. She could make time for someone else, and they could swap it with others who could then swap back with her: running her errands, fixing up her house. The crowd idling at the bus stop could put their skills to use: editing, darning, chopping vegetables, whatever they were best at; they'd add to their credit and, who knows, might find someone prepared to drive them to that meeting on the other side of town.

Of course, it didn't take long for the state to find out about the resistance and mount a response. Sometimes they'd go after the app designers, the strategists, pulling them in for questioning. Other times they targeted the money men, the people with small fortunes in time credits, emptying their accounts by detaining them and putting them in a semi-comatose state for days or even weeks, then dropping them off on the hard shoulder of rural highways. In a bid to lend the operation a more chilling, personal edge, one man was abducted on the eve of his wedding. He was drugged and slept for days, until his credit was exhausted, then his slumbering body was dumped on the outskirts of a deserted village.

Upon waking, he thought the world had come to an end.

It was around this time that Yehyia first met Hossam Yousry.

Hossam was having issues with his ID. The picture looked nothing like him. Or rather, it looked nothing like him *now*. It was an old photograph, taken just as Hossam was about to begin his military service, and in it he was thin and young with a full head of hair and the beginnings of a faint moustache—later mocked by the young woman he loved, and shamefacedly shaved clean. Unfortunately for Hossam, he was one of those people whose appearance can change overnight. Seven years had passed between the shutter's click and the day he presented himself to Yehyia: plump, prematurely gray, and smooth of chin and lip. With a little concentration, though, you could still see the resemblance between this man and the face: the eyes, though wearier, were unmistakable.

But to those at war with free time, to people like Yehyia, Hossam was the perfect target: he'd spent months and months trying to prove he was the rightful owner of his ID card simply so he could renew it. A single issue that had triggered problems in every part of his life—administrative difficulties leading to financial difficulties; trouble with the police; friction with the security services. And he was pretty much alone in life. His father was deceased, his older brother had gone abroad years before never to be heard from again, and only his blind, elderly mother was in his care. A gifted violinist, he'd been forced to take up work that was tantamount to begging, but even there the problem with the photo reared its head, and without family to vouch for the face on the card, he was left twisting in the wind. A pawn to be pushed around.

Yehyia could do nothing for him, and Hossam's file departed his desk as swiftly as it had arrived. Months later, though, he was back, and this time his face matched the photo exactly. A rigorous diet had restored his face's slenderness, his hair was coal black with dye, and the moustache was back. Moisturizers, diligently applied, reestablished his vanished youth.

A whole seven years younger. This was a serious matter; a grave threat. In one fell swoop, one man had won back two and a half thousand days of dead time. Would he mind waiting outside? They went into hasty conference, then emerged, smiling.

They took him to the department that was responsible for issuing IDs, sat him in front of the camera, and took his picture. The picture confirmed it: seven years younger.

At which moment, Hossam had a revelation. With the click of a shutter, these people had fixed him in time. He would have to be twenty years old forever: the same shameful moustache forever sprouting on his lip, the same inches forever kept off his waist, the same dye forever in his hair. He held up his new ID and peered at it: a passport to a past with no return. He thanked them with a curt nod and left.

That night, Yehyia couldn't sleep. He tossed and turned in bed until his wife lost her temper. *Here comes insomnia,* he said to himself, *I won't get to sleep for hours.* He found himself facing a sort of pure wakefulness he had never experienced. The next day on his way to work, he almost fell asleep in the car. A blare of horns startled him back to wakefulness. He was like that for the rest of the day, suspended between sleep and sleeplessness, and when it was time to go home he was too scared to drive, so he took a taxi instead. The driver had to shake him when they reached his street.

He ate early, a light supper, and laid down, but again, sleep defied him. That night he almost went mad. Consulted over the phone, a doctor friend suggested he take a pill, but it didn't work as intended, dragging him to sleep's threshold but not across it. And so on until morning, unable to tell whether he was asleep or awake. He called the friend again and arranged an appointment at the day clinic he ran at a private hospital.

This time he took the metro. He sat by the window. A gentle breeze ran over him and he sank into a deep, deep sleep.

He woke at the end of the line and caught a train back. He'd gone past the clinic and missed the appointment, but despite the seats being cramped and uncomfortable, he had recovered sufficiently to consider going to work. He gave himself a perfunctory wash in the office bathroom and went to his desk. He was in better shape than he had been the day before. He remembered that he'd left his car in the garage downstairs and drove it home. A couple of times he nearly dozed off, but managed to hold himself together.

Back upstairs to his apartment. No sleep again. The pills didn't help, nor the long hours he'd worked, nor the longer hours he lay prone beneath the air conditioner's lulling hum.

He made a note: sleep only came to him on the road, in transit.

He noted that the longer the road, the more soundly he slept.

He turned his day upside down. He left the house so early in the morning it was still night and caught the buses on their first empty runs around the city, the longest routes. He knew the metro network by heart. Telling himself that now he'd get some proper sleep for the first time in months, he bought a round trip ticket to Aswan. On the way, he lay in the train's sleeper cabin like it was a coffin: twelve hours of oblivion. He walked around the city till the return train was due, then slept all the way back to Cairo. He woke famished and for the first time in as long as he could remember he ate with genuine relish.

Back at home, as he lay bright-eyed on the bed beneath his wife's worried gaze, he knew that continuing his job—in any regular employment for that matter—was going to be impossible. He needed to stay on the highways and railway lines as much as possible. But with the exception of the Aswan train, there were no routes long enough to let him sleep his fill.

With all his days off claimed, there was nothing else to do: he had to resign. But what would he do if he quit his job? How would he survive?

Then one day he was asked to join a committee that was investigating a housing complaint.

He and his colleagues stood in the building in question. The residents said that the noise from the construction of the hotel next door was preventing them from sleeping. It made them neurotic, they said. Confused. They couldn't tell things apart anymore. Was their building going to be knocked down? Would they be compensated for the loss of their homes?

Yehyia couldn't hear anything much. *Maybe because it's daytime*, he thought. *Maybe it's worse at night.* Then he sat down, and as he sat he felt a strange peace. Something like tremors inside of him, like the vibrations in a train car. Like the apartment was rolling along on rails.

An inspector, asking to rent an apartment in the very building he was investigating. The residents were astonished.

His wife, of course, refused to move. He would visit her after work, then go back to the building. To the noise. To sleep. And that was where he told his story to the little stranger and his friend.

6

LOVE IS DEATH

– OR –

HOW I REALIZED I WASN'T IN LOVE WITH IRENE

Bahr said: "During my relationship with Irene, I fell in love with life again. For the first time in a long time, I stopped my obsessive fretting over death."

We were standing in New Square, watching a street artist sketch a young couple who stood frozen in place for the duration, their motionless lips parted in a pair of joyful smiles.

"Time was suddenly precious," said Bahr. "I loved life, like they say in songs. Which is why I started to suspect that it wasn't Irene I was in love with. An ex of mine had taught me that true love—or true happiness in love, rather—means you wouldn't mind dying right there and then, on the spot. And this, too: that you can love yourself and your lover, or you can love your lover and the time you spend together, or you can love yourself and the time you spend together. Like, in every relationship, there's a third wheel, which is time. And in my relationship with

Irene it was the third wheel that I loved.

"That said, love is a matter of degrees. With Irene, say, I was on the tenth floor of a skyscraper: far from the earth below, but further still from heaven."

The couple before us seemed enthusiastic despite their paralyzed pose, but for all the skill in her brush-work, the artist's movements were robotic and the smile of encouragement which she threw out from time to time seemed forced. Of course, that was only my impression. I could have been wrong. We watched them all for a while—the painter, the couple, the canvas—then we moved on.

Bahr was still talking:

Maybe that's why it all ended one freezing morning at a deserted lake. The tears that came to my eyes that day didn't come from inside. They were more like smoke, smoke from the cigarettes we tried as teenagers before we knew to draw it down into our lungs, leaving it to drift and spill from our noses and throats. What does it say about all the joys we shared, the walks and the films and the celebrations, if at the end of it all I couldn't summon a single heartfelt tear?

And what about the games I played with little Adam? I could see him in my mind's eye as I stood there by the lake. Like he was like a little doll. The world was suddenly unreal. Adam and Irene and I were unreal. Put it like this: keeping a bag by the front door had done something to my heart; there was some flaw in there that stopped it from working as it should. Anxiety eating away at the walls of its chambers like water at rock. A quick glance tells you nothing's happening, but it is.

That day, I sat at the side of the road by the lapping edge of the lake and bid farewell to the life I'd entrusted to those two bodies: one soft and strong, the other small. My past is full of people left behind, buried bodies. I'd never wept before. I had forgotten how life could be. I had settled down, fallen into that love of mine, and hadn't run when the running was good. Now life's hammer had come down right where I stood and had moved me on despite myself.

So I moved on. But Adam and Irene are still with me, the silent, invisible audience that accompanies me everywhere I go. They watch me wordlessly, perhaps waiting for me to shed a tear at last. Where I live now there's this bakery that looks just like the place where Irene used to work. I'll buy a few pastries from the women there and imagine that they are her coworkers, that they are sizing me up. I'll sit down to eat, trying to look unhappier than I actually am. It's the thought of that ice creeping back over my face that alarms me. That it will hide the emotions I want to convey.

It was the lack of expression that first attracted her to me. The combination of a scowl and dark skin had been too much for her to resist, she'd whisper. From the moment she left her village for the city where we met, she had been working. Tirelessly and lovelessly. The day I first ordered food from her, then pointedly ordered more, she made up her mind that she would respond to my advances; she would take that step, she told herself; she wouldn't be a cog in a machine anymore.

And that, Seif, as you know yourself by now, was her mistake.

More importantly, though, it was my mistake, because I already knew that when a man stops moving he puts himself in the hands of fate. Life's wave will snatch you and drag you out to sea, and when it's done with you, when it's washed you up, a bundle on a beach, every bone in your body will be broken. But then again, who could have resisted? Blue-eyed in a foreign bakery.

Well, that's a slightly strange way to put it: every bakery over there is foreign. I don't mean it like that. In the village where I grew up there was this place called the foreign bakery. It made the soft white rolls called fino, and was across the road from the ovens of the traditional bakery that turned out the rough flat discs of baladi bread. In their homes, most women still baked the huge, heavy loaves which sometimes had the buttery taste of fateer. Then the women realized that the foreign bakery could save them the effort of making Eid cookies. They would drop off empty trays in the morning, and send their kids to collect them, fully laden, that evening.

The bakery was the site of my first attempt to meddle with fate. We children were hanging around, waiting for the cookies, and the women working there asked us to help them pack the little fino rolls into bags and tie them shut. Five fino rolls in a bag was called a kaiser. So, I decided that I was going to spread a little joy among my fellow villagers. In every other bag I stuffed an extra roll or two. In the days that followed, I made the rounds of the local stores supplied by the bakery, buying myself a kaiser to take to school, in hope of finding one of the bonus bags I'd packed. But I never came across a single one, and I started to wonder whether the whole thing hadn't been a dream or an illusion, the way it always feels when you do (or imagine you are doing) somebody a favor—especially somebody you don't know... But look at where my thoughts have taken me, look at where I've taken you. Poor Irene left standing there, waiting patiently for this idle talk to end...

Irene was, without a shadow of a doubt, the best thing in that bakery. I had been in the country for years by then, but was still having difficulties with my papers. Plus, I had a bit of cash saved up from all the different jobs I'd done. You might say that circumstance conspired against us; that it laid a trap and in we fell. Or in I fell, I should say, because I knew it was a trap. Irene, though: How could she ever have known?

Whatever the case, we met our punishment together. See how purely evil life can be?

All I said was: "Morning, miss. You're beautiful."

She stared, then smiled: "What would you like?"

"A date."

The smile in her eyes turned to cheerful contempt. At the window, death peered in. Fresh victims. But he was happy to wait until the two of us had become three.

We walked to the farthest edge of New Square, to the barbed wire, where the soldiers lounged dreamily atop their armored cars. We didn't approach them, nor did the silence of the alleyways behind them encourage it.

Bahr was still speaking, and I wondered: *If motherhood is an instinct, something bred in the bone, then what is fatherhood?*

My understanding—and it might not fit with everyone's experience—is that fatherhood is a life rinsed clean. Like laundered money. Here are your genes, washed spotless, reborn and innocent. Here you are, with one sacred duty: care for this delicate creature who relies on you entirely; who has no other father in the world but you. What a bond!

You can outwit yourself like that. When part of you starts thinking about all the mistakes you've made, when it sounds the alarm and says, "Flee!" then you offer an argument in mitigation: your child. Let's wait until the kid's raised and grown, and can (How do they put it? That's right:) look after himself.

My argument, my pretext for not killing myself, my fresh start, was a boy named Adam. Irene and I chose a name that both of us could pronounce. I waited impatiently for what I never got: his first word. I wanted to know how he'd say it; how his tongue would blend his parents'. But before he could gather those first sounds into words, it was over. Those effortful syllables, that face which bore the faint shadow of my own dark skin—these are my entire memory of him. A bird-call voice singing scattered signs, exquisite little lips that sucked at my neck as I held him, like he was sipping milk through my skin. Wide blue eyes like Irene's.

Life played a smarter hand this time. Two birds with one stone. It used me to prove its point.

For the first two years everything went well—the relationship, the pregnancy, the birth—and it felt as though my old life were nothing but a story, a lie someone told me a hundred years ago. Sometimes I would wake in the middle of the night with an inexplicable panic, in a cold sweat, but without any memory of having dreamed. Maybe I hadn't. But the things I knew, the blows I kept waiting to fall—they ran their fingers over my body as I slept. They ravaged me.

When the blow finally came, it was in the form of a boy, a teenager who harassed Irene on her way to work. Wolf whistles, obscenities, and racism. Irene was an outsider twice over. First, because she came from a village; second, because she was living with a black man. He'd make comments about her milk-white breasts, and always, whether she walked away or turned to shout at him, he'd call her "black man's bitch."

We lived a fair distance from the city center and, back then at least, especially in suburbs like ours, the police were not overly zealous about such things. Particularly since we didn't know the boy's name or where he lived. The neighborhood was full of kids his age, roaming in packs. Plus, I only found out about it all much later, when Irene burst into tears one night and woke me up. It was just before dawn.

That morning, I went with her. The boy didn't show. Nor the next day. We finally saw him on the third day. Very tall and slim, sitting on the low wall that ran beside a little lake. The lake was always deserted in the mornings, but on holidays and weekends it was packed with people lounging on the grass. I wanted to go up to him, but Irene held me back. "There's no need," she said. "He's seen you with me, and now he'll be too scared to do it again." I was a young man back then: short for sure, but I had a broad chest and a look about me. I was only a few years older than him. He didn't say anything, just stared.

For the next few days, I went with Irene to work and the boy didn't show again. I'd take her to the bakery, come home to sleep for another hour, then drop Adam off with the daughter of one of our neighbors before walking to work at the paint shop. If there was any work to be had.

Irene seemed happier, and happier with me, but a couple of days later her expression fell again. I decided to put an end to it once and for all. At this juncture you might well ask, "How is it your deep understanding of the laws of life didn't make you better at breaking them? Didn't help you outmaneuver them?" Well, I knew something bad was coming, but I couldn't resist. That night, as I lay down beside Irene, my heart was beating so hard it shook my whole body.

The next morning, I kissed Irene and told her I had to be off. I'd had a job that started early. She gave me a worried look. She said, "Look after yourself, my love." I kissed her again.

I didn't kiss Adam because I didn't want him to wake up. I left. I never saw them again.

Walking down to the lake, I realized that I was clenching my right fist, hard. There was no one there when I arrived, but then I heard a whispering. It was coming from behind a steel-panel fence and I went over to see. The boy was sitting behind the fence, and with him was a young woman about the same age. They were smoking something.

I stood and watched them for a while and was making to leave when the boy saw me and called out in a slushy voice, "Heeeeey! Blackie!"

I stopped.

"Where's your bitch?"

The girl was staring at me quizzically, but when the boy added, "Bring the bitch! We're fine with threesomes here!" she burst out laughing.

Whatever he was smoking had taken it out of him, so it wasn't that hard to get him on the ground. I'd left the house intending to teach him a lesson, to give him a beating, drawing on the rage I felt at Irene's tears, but who can say with any certainty what will happen even a minute from now?

He was on his back, on the lakeshore grass, and I was on top of him, each with our hands at the other's neck, when suddenly I felt his girlfriend grip my throat from behind and squeeze. They were both choking me and all I could do—levering as much strength as I could from the base of my spine—was squeeze harder myself. I saw his eyes bulge and for a split second I had a vision of both of us dead, locked together, with the bitch on my back the only survivor.

I once read that, for over ninety percent of people imprisoned for murder or manslaughter—for killing someone—it was their first and only offense. Most were completely ordinary people who, for a brief moment, brushed up against something outside this world—an instant in which they were turned into instruments for death—then the moment passed, leaving them beached, ordinary once more, gaping in astonishment at their victim's corpse and trying to summon them back to life as though that death, too, might only be momentary.

In that moment on the lakeshore, as I throttled him, as they throttled me, I remembered:

One night, while I was being interrogated following my arrest at the demonstration, the officer made a strange request.

I was blindfolded, being escorted from one interrogation room to another. They were pushing me down a corridor when I heard a sound off to one side, like the repeated banging of some metallic object. My blindfold was jerked up and the officer said, "Kill it."

I looked and I saw it: a rat in a trap.

The tinny banging I'd heard was the sound of the rat throwing itself against the metal bars of its cage.

My eyes were still adjusting to the light and of course I had no idea how I was going to kill the thing.

How do you even get at a rat in a cage? I stood facing the rat, bewildered.

Then the officer was pointing at a bucket of water. "Drown it, you idiot."

I didn't understand what was going on. This didn't seem like any kind of torture, not even an attempt to teach me a lesson. It didn't seem like anything, just an order; only, I had no idea why.

I'd never killed a rat before. I kneeled by the little cage and reached my hand out cautiously, scared of its bite. But the rat was far more scared than I was. It pushed itself into the far corner of its cage and glared at me out of one terror-stricken eye.

Gingerly, with the tips of my fingers, I lifted the trap. *Drop it in the bucket and walk away,* I told myself. And if they didn't let me walk away then I'd shut my eyes and try not to look.

I dropped the cage and turned away. But the bucket was narrower than I'd assumed and the corner of the cage stuck on the lip of the bucket, preventing it from sinking all the way. Most of the cage was underwater, then, but that uppermost corner was still clear, and there the rat clung to the bars, shuddering hysterically, pushing his snout between them.

I stared at the rat. I didn't know what to do. After a few moments, the officer glanced over at me and laughed. He said, "You don't know how to kill it, sweetheart?"

He pointed to a second bucket. "Tip that over it."

I lifted the second bucket and began to pour water over the rat's protruding nose. The force of the

falling water pushed the rat off the bars. The officer
barked at me not to waste water. "Don't spill a drop,"
he said. I continued to pour: a steady stream whenever the rat poked his head back up. The rat was trying and trying to push his head against the stream,
but couldn't, and now the water was exactly level
with the lip of the first bucket and the rat's nose
was millimeters beneath the surface. A little while
longer and it gave up altogether. Stopped moving
and sank.

The officer turned away, one of the guards hitched
the blindfold back down over my eyes, and they took
me to my cell.

On the shore of that lake in Europe, wrestling that
boy, I remembered the rat.

How old was the boy? Seventeen, perhaps. Or
eighteen. Nineteen? Whatever it was, that was as
old as he'd get. Suddenly, the silence was absolute. I
turned, but the girl was nowhere to be found. When
I turned back, the body that seconds before had been
locked in combat with me was completely motionless.

Looking back on that silence, its sudden settling,
I feel nothing more acutely than the fragility of our
existence—how out of place my pride and anger suddenly seemed.

But in the moment, that morning, I wasn't so
philosophical. My neck was agony and I felt half-
dead. Everything else was unchanged—the water, the
grass, the still trees, the morning birds—and as I lay
there I pictured Irene and Adam asleep in bed, and I

knew that I would never see either of them again, and it seemed perfectly fair.

Wait. You thought I'd killed them, didn't you? When I told you I'd buried bodies, you thought I meant it literally. Seif, you have to learn how to deal with metaphors. Their tangle is so much closer to the truth than our reality.

I looked down at the boy. Weren't corpses meant to be open-eyed; like, death's blank stare? So why did this one have its eyes shut? I felt the brief ghost of a hope that he wasn't dead. I shook him, slapped him, thumped his chest. I parted his teeth and breathed down his throat. I did everything I had ever seen or heard or read about. How long was I at it? Ten seconds? An hour? Only the trees in their silent vigil know.

As I kneeled there, desperate, despairing, I heard a distant voice call out, then a distant scream. I got to my feet, knowing that I must run again. This time, even from my name. So I ran, and I never found out what happened to the boy, or to Irene and Adam. Soon after I left, there was a civil war in that country, an ethnic conflict, and not a stone or a soul was left untouched. Years later, I saw a photograph in a newspaper of what could easily have been the neighborhood where we'd lived, and I couldn't help but think I could see the spot where our home had been, except it was just a heap of stones, piled up like on a grave. And I wondered: If life had punished *me* for stopping so long in this place, if it had torn down everything *I'd* built, what was that boy being punished for? Not for his insolence, surely: life doesn't care about that. Who knows? Maybe for nothing more than sitting in the same place so often, down by the lake.

7

PERMISSION

They didn't wait long. They went with him to her burial, held back a few days, then shyly returned to his front door.

At first, Ahmed kept to himself, shut up at home, but eventually he emerged to face them. He almost asked them outright: "So how did you all manage before the visions?" He was sure that they were going to question him, to ask his advice on the details of their lives, the way they'd questioned his father through his mother. But they surprised him. The elders assembled before him and said they *did* want to ask his advice (or rather, they wanted to ask his father's advice— that is, if he was in contact) but only concerning one, very important, matter.

This was when he learned of Salem's return.

They told him of Salem's offer, about the boat and the group discount, and then they paused. Did he remember Salem?

No, he didn't remember Salem, why? Never mind, they said. Listen, they said. They'd been thinking about leaving. All of them. All of them meaning all of them, meaning every single one. At first he was taken aback, then he was curious, then he thought to himself how strange it would be to face death with the people you'd lived with all your life. They had made up their minds, they explained, but they wanted to hear what his father had to say. A final opinion. They were going to start getting ready, but would be waiting for his response. If he wouldn't mind?

Ahmed heard himself promising them an answer.

He closed the door behind him. The walls were silent and told him nothing. That night he slept in his parents' old room, but all his dreams were of the sea and childhood.

A few nights later he left the house and walked out of the village. Nothing to see but a handful of stars in the sky above and gravestones looming in the moonlight, where his mother and father lay silent forever. He wandered into the cemetery, but his heart clenched in his chest and he retreated. Then he dozed for a while, though didn't notice he had dozed. And no one came by, not as he slept, not while he was awake. He liked it: the solitude, the comfort of silence.

His second night out he met a traveler at the primitive tea stall out by the highway. The server had gone to sleep and the makeshift stall in its thicket of palms seemed deserted, but the traveler had tied up his donkey and was sprawled out on the wooden bench. Ahmed asked the man where he was going, and the man asked Ahmed why he was wandering around at night. He was hoping to see his father, Ahmed said. The man asked why he didn't go to the wall of visions—the one down south. The man said this quite simply, like he was talking about the kaaba or the pyramids, yet this was the first time Ahmed had ever heard of the wall.

He asked the permission of the village elders, though he didn't tell them where he was going, then he rode the train south and climbed the hillside. The day dawned over him and his fellow seekers after visions, and he watched as they stared and wept and sighed and called out the names of their loved ones. But all he could see was the sun's glare off the rock. Then the sun departed and the people with it. He stayed on two nights more, but nothing came of it, like he was the only blind man among them.

Back to Wahda, his hopes dashed. When he arrived, it felt like things were missing. A lot of things. There were no cars or carts, no trash in heaps, no children's toys; it was as though some gigantic hand had reached down and swept through the village streets, wiping them clean. When the elders came to him that evening he still didn't know what he'd say.

He welcomed them in. Stared at his feet. Then he heard himself speak: "I saw my father walking on water, laughing, and I saw us following him."

Joy and resolve gleamed in the eyes of those assembled, and each man rose and went away to spend their final nights at home.

On the appointed night, they went down to the sea, and Ahmed went with them. On the outskirts of the village he paused to help two young men uproot the sign and smear it with dirt.

They camped on the shore, and when the boat came they all climbed in, Ahmed and the young men helping the elderly and children aboard, but by the time the anchor was raised he had vanished into the darkness. Deep in a stand of palms he watched the boat pull away, laden with people and memories: a little nation riding the waves. He noticed that none of them looked back.

He didn't go back to the abandoned village. He went farther: back to the hillside in the deep south with its hidden wall. Not praying for guidance this time, but for confirmation. A sign from his father that he hadn't sent them to their destruction. He wanted a nod, a smile, some small gesture free of disapproval. Unlike the other pilgrims to the wall, he stayed, assisting visitors like a devotee at a saint's shrine, and still he saw nothing, and still he didn't know why. And then one day, the two strangers came, and they saw. Or at least one of them did, then slept. The older man, the little one, was scribbling things down and looking around. He even told Ahmed his story. But as for the younger man, well, he was fast asleep, absent from this world and motionless, without the slightest tremor stirring him, and this was the sign that he'd seen.

8

BRIGHT PAINT ON GRAY GROUND

– OR –

YOU TOO ARE AFRICAN

Mere hours before the ship that was supposed to take me back home departed, I sat, drinking glass after glass with a Moroccan.

The ground was rocky, just like this, but covered with a light grass. We were sitting, the superstructures of container ships looming in the port nearby, time running slowly away like water from a leaking flask. With every drop of brandy I grew lazier and more indifferent, and when the clock struck ten in the morning it was too late to change my mind even if I'd wanted to. I watched my ship depart and then draw away. I thought I could hear it sounding its whistle, a great whistling, and I thought I could hear the whistle crying out my name: Bahr! Bahr!

The ship departed, and I watched it go from the grass where I sat, and it was as though I were watching my life drawing away: my past, and everything

I had ever known; my country, slipping away like a wave runs back from the rocks to rejoin the great body of water at its back.

When I was a young man, the idea of traveling to Europe to find work had come easy. I'd known for certain that I was never coming back. It wasn't a question of making a decision to stay, though. It was a feeling: blood thrilling to see the ship go back without me. I knew I was going to have to disappear for a long time, that I would suffer and go on suffering, but as long as I was away from this shithouse of a country, none of that mattered.

There was a rush of courage from the brandy. I pulled a lighter from my pocket, flicked out a flame, and with my free hand I raised my passport aloft, bulky and leaden like a disaster. I spoke aloud: "Fire purges everything."

As Bahr spoke, it was as though the tang of saltwater rose off his story, not blown in from the shore nearby where the reeds were being battered about in the wind. There was no one around, though they had told us this was where all the boats set out; that it was from this thin spit of sand that Wahda had slipped away. I was silent, full of a heavy gloom that had descended when he'd told me the story of the boy. The boy he thought he'd killed.

I didn't know then that his end was near, that he wouldn't be coming back with me.

In the two silences—my silence and the silence of the sea that lay behind the faint wash of its

waves—Bahr told me what came next, during his first
days of running from the boy beside the lake:

I stayed in a refugee camp for a while with two other
men, one Eastern European, the other Asian. The
laundry block was on the camp's perimeter. It was always full of clothes, but you never saw anyone there:
as though they were coming in camouflaged, chame-
leons. And the dryers were always full, too. Often, I'd
have to hang my clothes out on a line. One day, I
went in to collect my dry clothes, but I couldn't find
them amid the chaos of linen and nylon. "They're
over there." It was a young man, pointing casually:
"There." I couldn't believe it. How had he managed
to pick them out like that? And then, after standing
and puzzling for a while, I started to see that almost
all the clothes littering the room were plain black
or blue, while my shirts and shorts were white and
blue, red and yellow; were striped and spotted. Like
bright paint spilled on a gray ground; scarlet daubed
on black. And in that moment, as I gazed down at
the gaudy display, I was brought back to my dark
continent. I remembered how we used to watch the
African refugees in their brightly patterned clothes,
how we used to laugh and mock and stare. I remembered the silent football team I told you about. I did
tell you about that, didn't I?

In any case, it hadn't occurred to me that I was
on the same stretch of European coastline where I'd
gotten drunk with my Moroccan friend some thirty
years before. Back to the coast, a foreigner no more.

Was it really the same place, though, or did it just look the same? I was sitting by myself this time. It was morning, and I had a can of beer in my hand. I was screwing the other cans into the sand to keep them cold, when I saw something being carried up the beach toward me on the waves. It came to rest at my feet. Something wooden; a primitive toy eaten away by the salt. For the first time in years, my heart was beating hard.

It was a little wooden doll. Where I come from they called them samannous. Girls used to play with them—they were made from the cane that was used to make flutes. The cane was painted red and yellow, then locks of real hair, usually their mother's, was stuck on its doum-nut head. Inside the hollowed nut, a folded scrap of paper was tucked: a charm to shield the girl from evil, from devils, from strangers.

I picked the samannous up and examined it in the red glow that climbed from the horizon. Then I turned to the sea, and just beyond the line where the first waves gathered to run in, I saw something bobbing in the water. I heard the growl of an outboard motor. A naval launch, heading for the object. From where I stood I couldn't tell what exactly they lifted out of the water, but it quickly became clear that, whatever it was, it was only the beginning. Suddenly, the sea was full of them, surfacing like bubbles then slowly, slowly, washing in on the tide, and if the wooden doll had told me something, the smell that now filled my lungs told me everything. Bright colors, bobbing in the surf, brought me back to what I

had forgotten. The first sign that I would return. That
I would make the trip back *here*.

Along the shore where Bahr and I were sitting, sandgrouse swooped to earth. They would dive in, then
stop abruptly and hang there, frozen in midair. As the
light grew stronger we made out the net strung between two poles. Eager and inexperienced, the birds
were snarling in the fine lines of its mesh.

9

WHAT'S LOST IN SLEEP

In the little hotel where we were staying, in the closest town to the smugglers' beach, I opened my eyes and tried the phone again. Then again. After repeated attempts I found a faint signal, and a notification informed me that I had received several calls from a single number: Leila. My heartbeat quickened as I thought back to the missed calls on that other, distant day, and I tried calling her. No answer, so I called the magazine, where they asked me to hold. Seconds later her voice came through the line and I breathed again. "Are you all right?" she asked, urgency in her voice.

My misgivings returned. "Why, what is it?"

"All these people came to the office yesterday, asking about you and Bahr. We told them you hadn't been in for a while and they left without leaving their names. They seemed worried."

I said, "Well, I'll ask Bahr. Maybe he knows who they are."

There was a moment's silence, then Leila said, "Please take care. Things aren't great here, you know."

I asked her what she meant. "Just take care," she said, and I felt a stinging in the corner of my eye. I thanked her and hung up.

Suddenly, I remembered something that had happened the night before. I'd been woken by the sound of banging. Like someone banging on the wall. I'd assumed it was a dream, and maybe it had been, but now I wasn't so sure.

I told Bahr about the call and he seemed worried, more worried than I thought he'd be. He took his bag from behind the door and asked me to get mine. We left the hotel in a hurry.

Outside, we stood at the line where the palms met the desert. We waited there until a taxi came by that seemed robust enough to manage the whole route. The sun was racing into the heart of the sky as we drove away.

A few hours later the engine cut out and refused to restart. The driver said he'd have to get help. We looked around. There was nothing: no shops, no cafés, no garages. We told the driver that we'd go with him. "You won't be able to walk all that way in the sun," he said, and with those words, to our astonishment, he left us, drawing away until he was just a point in the distance and winking out.

There we were, all alone. We sat speechless in the back of the car: no water, no food, no reception on the phones. An hour passed, two, and the sun began its return to earth. We decided to walk.

We got out, and walked until the roughly laid road disappeared and we were surrounded by a landscape of scrub and sand. Bahr said that we should stay where we were and wait for someone to come by; we didn't want to get lost in the desert.

So we sat, slouched against our bags. We began to grow drowsy and Bahr stretched out on the ground. "We'll go on when we wake up," he said.

But the drowsiness was a mirage. We didn't sleep, and out of the blue, Bahr decided to answer my question:

"I didn't choose you, Seif."

He said nothing for a moment, then continued, "I didn't ask for you to come with me. Truth is, I'd never heard of you, never read anything you'd written. I didn't know you. Leila vouched for you, but she didn't pick you, either. She told me about you—about what you've kept hidden from me—and I worked out the rest. You seemed perfect for the trip. Like you were closing a circle that had been broken since the day my eyes first opened on the world."

He turned to me.

"Why did you switch your phone off, Seif? The day of that business with Alya? Did you know?

"Let me tell you what I think. I think you expected it. Deep down, you knew what was going to happen. You knew that all that joy and celebration was just an illusion, that they'd never surrender so easily. That if they *did* surrender, then first they'd have their revenge. In a way, you deserve my congratulations. You turned your phone off at the perfect moment—just after you'd made sure that she thought you were out there on the street. A hero in the midst of battle. Bravo, Seif. A proper bastard. A bona fide runaway. Just like me."

I gaped at him, half questioning, half taken aback.

"I've never forgotten that boy at the lake, but later I witnessed crimes for which there are no punishments under any law. For instance, no one's going to throw you in prison because you turned your partner's life into a hell of jealousy, resentment, and insecurity. No one's going to lock you up because you did precisely what was required to drive those closest to you mad, or because you hid yourself away while people believed you were at the forefront of the battle. Or because you acted in a way that terrified the people who had opened their doors to you, who had lowered their defenses."

Silence reigned once more. Dozens of questions rose to my tongue and died there. Bahr's head lolled between his hunched shoulders, and, with astonishing self-possession, he began to doze.

I looked around us. Evening was falling. It felt like the stars could hear my heart. *When I get back,* I thought, *I have questions for Leila. If I get back.* And I told myself it was the fear that kept sleep so far away, much further even than the far edge of this desert.

But then, suddenly, I was waking up. The light in the sky was like dawn, and I knew I had slept for many hours.

You sleep heavier than the night itself. That's what Alya used to say to me, and now, waking, the very moment I opened my eyes, I remembered everything. There was nobody there, and nothing.

All alone, without my bag, without papers. I was alone, without Bahr.

The phone in my pocket a silent corpse.

I got to my feet, still caught between sleep and the day, and began to move, to wander, to circle myself. Nothing but silence and sand.

There were tracks in the sand, many and intersecting, but who was I to tell what caused them? I saw dark stains soaked into the dust, and prayed they weren't blood. Was I obligated to picture the horrors that might have played out here, or must I doubt Bahr himself? A thought no less horrifying at first, but its sting faded as the minutes passed. Hunger pinched, but the light was growing brighter. A breeze I felt as faint hope sprang up and I began to move again.

10

THE HIDDEN HEART

Back home, I tossed and turned, caught between sleep and waking, between life and death.

A truck saved me, one of the huge container trucks transporting water between the desert towns. Peering down at me from his cab, the driver's expression reminded me of the look on the streetcar driver's face the day I stood back-to-back with Bahr in Alexandria, but unlike the streetcar driver, this man had braked to a halt, opened the passenger-side door, and motioned me over. I heaved myself up and in and was about to strike up a conversation when I simply dropped out of the waking world.

"If sleep were an ocean, then you'd drown, because you're heavier."

That was what Alya used to say.

I'd respond, "I sleep so soundly because you're here."

The driver dropped me off at the outskirts of the

city and warned me to take care. The troubles had returned and the streets weren't safe. The authorities had imposed a curfew.

The streets were perhaps a little less crowded than usual, that was all. I chased the fleeing remnants of daylight and bought myself a sandwich from the place outside my building. My blue car sat there, unloved but unstolen beneath heaped dust. Up the stairs to my apartment. I looked through my pockets for the keys and couldn't find them, so I first pushed on the door, then kicked. Despite the noise, the neighbors' doors stayed closed. Then mine splintered at the lock and gave way. I went in, propped it shut with a chair, and went to sleep.

The power was out when I woke up. Groping around in the darkness, my hands found the sandwich and I gobbled it down. Feeling my blood pressure plummet I lay back down. Then I tried calling Leila, but I remembered that I hadn't charged my phone, so I tried my landline. There was no response: from Leila or anybody else. I drifted off again.

The power was still out the next morning. I fetched a stack of loose paper and sat down to write what I'd seen, the paper piling up beside me like I was two people not one, and the hours ticking past, racing me.

The sun was setting—though the light was still like early morning—when there was a knock at the door. A knock I knew from long ago. Then the door began to open tentatively, scraping the chair back, and Leila eased through. She set her bag down on the floor, and sat. For a moment she said nothing, then, "I found this outside the door."

She bent and took a little tin box from her bag, about the size of an old-fashioned candy tin. She sighed, gripped the edge of the lid, and popped it open. She didn't take her eyes off me.

I looked inside. The box was full of sheets of paper, something gray, and then, resting on top of it all, a pair of red glasses.

I stared. Mouthed a whisper: "Bahr!"

Then I drifted off again. Then woke again. Evening spilled into the living room, filling it to the brim. Leila was reading by the light of a candle. I squinted to make sure she was really there, and I wished that we could stay like this forever. She sensed my stirring.

"The power's out."

"Where did you get that candle?"

"Everyone carries candles these days." She jerked her thumb at the door: "Why'd you leave it open?"

I looked at the door through the room's gloom and saw it had been propped shut with the chair once again. Then I looked for the tin, but couldn't see it. Leila turned back to the pages I had written, read for a while, then raised her head.

"Do these places really exist? Did you really meet these people?"

I didn't answer.

She glanced back down, smiling uncertainly. "And who's this Bahr?"

She looked straight at me.

"Seif... Do you still see the dead?"

AFTERWORD

1

TRAIN IN MY HEAD

"I couldn't feel my body, but I could tell that I was naked," Alya said. "And I could see them beneath the spotlight: the heads, talking at me through white masks; the gesturing hands. All I could hear was a train.

"The sound of a heavy train rolling slowly over old rails—a steady clack-clack—and I sensed it was carrying me away, someplace quiet. I knew that they were talking to me and that they were smiling behind their masks, though how I knew I couldn't say. And through it all the sound of the train was very strong and very present in the theater. I tried lifting my head, craning my neck to watch the train go by. The train was gold, with a ridiculous wooden smokestack like something from a cartoon, but though I felt my head was raised, that I was watching that train, I hadn't moved at all. I'm not sure if it's possible to describe the feeling, but it was as if I were walking up a down escalator, moving or sitting in a waiting room where time itself had been switched off. That's how it was for me, unable to move, unable to speak. Then someone put something over my face, over my nose and mouth, and said, 'Count to ten.' And I hadn't counted at all, when suddenly… Tik! Tak!"

Alya paused for a moment, then went on.

"No, that was it exactly: Tik! Tak! They put me under and woke me up. Killed me and brought me back. Just like that. Tik! Then, tak! Like they'd pushed a button or something. Like I was a vacuum cleaner."

She turned to me, "Do you think I'm a vacuum cleaner?"

I grinned despite myself.

"I do not."

"No, that's *exactly* what I am. They pushed the button twice. Killed me and revived me. Like gods, or God's emissaries."

She paused. What she said next was the sort of thing that Bahr would be telling me just two years later.

"But if they were sent by God they wouldn't have come so late. Why didn't He send them earlier? And if they were gods, why couldn't they have been gentler with me? Or is it just that He or they don't care?"

"I don't know," I said. "I haven't heard from Him in a long time. Maybe it's you who should be telling me. You're the one with supernatural talents. I'm the only earthling here."

She didn't smile. "We still don't know…" she said, looking down at herself, her body beneath the bandages.

"I'll leave here missing parts of myself. I wonder what else got pulled out with my womb."

Another pause, like she was facing the truth all over again. I didn't volunteer a response.

She clearly made a great many decisions in the days that followed. She didn't tell me any of this, not in so many words, but it was clear enough from her behavior. And as the weeks went by, her reticence took on the solidity of fact. To repeat, nothing was said, but even so I began to think of my fingers—in my dream, in the moment they'd let her slip away from me—as somehow criminal, and her aloofness as her punishment.

In an attempt to get her back, I suggested she come and work at the magazine as a translator. "Use your languages." She came, and very quickly settled in, but in ways that could only be sensed, not seen, her reticence continued. One day I came in to find her clutching that old edition of the magazine, the one the revolutionaries had trampled into the streets and that I'd thought was gone forever. She had it open on the article I had written at the editor's request. Was actually reading it. When she sensed me standing there, she looked up, and casually flipped the page. She was on the verge of saying something, but instead she just pressed her lips tight, dropped the magazine on the chair, and walked out, leaving me standing by that window, looking out over the trees.

2

BESIDE A TREMBLING CANDLE

I said to Leila, "Stay here tonight."

"I only came to check on you," she said. She held my gaze a beat longer, then rose.

"My friend lives nearby. Can you take me there, Seif?"

"The car's dead."

She smiled, "I don't think I've ever seen it alive. Anyway, my friend's too close to drive."

She beat me to the front door; I followed her out.

We were at her friend's place in no time. On the way, Leila kept trying her number but there was no reception. Before she went upstairs she said, "Just wait here for five minutes. In case no one's in."

I waited in the lobby, peering up the stairwell. Suddenly, Leila was there.

"Looks like she's out."

The streetlight's gleam in her eyes was the edge of a memory, and I trembled.

Pull yourself together.

I asked, "Are you still in that place on the other side of town?"

She nodded but said nothing.

"Then let's go back to mine then."

Again, she nodded, and it looked like despair. On the way back she walked next to me in silence, and for the first time I found myself wondering if losing Alya could put everything right.

We were unaware that the curfew had already started until we saw the cars jockeying, racing to get home. Up ahead, two armored cars were rolling steadily toward us down the street, each blocking a lane.

Leila clutched at my hand; we turned and jogged quickly across Talaat Harb toward Abdeen, but there, too, our way was blocked by armored cars and soldiers. They waved us back. So we turned down Qahqary Street and into the alleys that link Gawad Hosni with Sherif and Qasr El Nil. On either side, barbed wire was being rolled out to block off Qasr El Nil, and my eye was caught by the towering bulk of a half-built hotel, then the weary lean of the building next to it, and I said to Leila, "I know that building."

We went straight in through the front doors. No one was in the lobby and we began to climb the stairs. The doors were all shut fast and the deathly quiet made the apartments seem abandoned. Fleetingly, I wondered whether the residents had passed away. On we climbed, up the spiral staircase until we came to the room on the roof where Bahr and I had spoken to the neurotic tenant, what seemed like an eternity ago. I knocked and the door inched open. I pushed and we went in.

There was no one there. As we looked out through the wide window onto the square—distant and shuttered and dark—I told Leila that the last time I had come here, with Bahr, the building had been full of residents. In the light from the huge hotel next door, lit up but silent, I saw her watching me with an expression that ranged between doubt, anxiety, and trust.

She reached out and took my hand. She said, "Let me tell you something…" She paused.

"Let's say the whole thing is what I think it is. That you've been writing a story, a fiction. I'm talking about Bahr and the expedition. All that."

She fell silent again. When she resumed, she was trying to smile:

"Thank you for giving me a part in it."

And before I could answer, the roaring began.

3

MALFUNCTION

Only once did I get the chance to look through Bahr's notes. He had gone with Yehyia to look around the department and left me waiting in a café on the corner of Gomhouriya Street. More importantly, he had left his bag with me, and had left it only half-closed, too. Through the unzipped opening I could see the words *The End Days* at the head of a sheet of paper. I slid it out carefully and began to read:

The end times will begin with a barber slitting the throat of the customer lying supine between his hands; with a butcher letting his hand carry the cleaver right through the meat and into the shoppers clustered around the flyblown flesh. Drivers will lurch through red lights and mow pedestrians down. Mothers will follow through on the threats and actually sit on their children; whores will crush johns' balls between their thighs; electricians will cross wires, galvanizing whole apartments, whole buildings; at day's end, sewer workers will remove manhole covers, converting them into death traps in the dark; carpenters will make merry with their saws, blacksmiths with their hammers. The doctor will plunge his syringe into the patient's eyes; the taxi driver will snap his wheel off as the passengers scream. Police officers and guards will be seized by a compulsion to empty every last round from their magazines, their fizzing bullets finding silence in the bodies they strike. On the crowded buses, passengers' hands will reach out to throttle their neighbors with belts and cords. Those lounging on the corniche walls will have hands propel them down into the river or the sea. Trucks will roll at top speed over the cracking shells of cars. Cranes and excavators will whirl like fans, laying waste. Peasants' mattocks will stick in necks not soil.

4

THE RETURN

After a few seconds, it became apparent to both Leila and me that the shaking wasn't simply an illusion created by the noise. The windowpanes shook, the lightbulbs swung on the ceiling, the chairs jitterbugged. It was like a little earthquake was playing with us. I went to the window, and I looked down, and I saw.

Endless ranks of people, coming down the street with a slow, heavy tramp that set everything swaying. I couldn't make out faces in the darkness, and there were no signs, no chants, but even so there was something familiar about this crowd, something I couldn't explain.

I turned to Leila and saw, to my surprise, that a streak of gray had appeared in her hair. Then I noticed the fine powder that billowed and floated from the ceiling and walls, the particles swirling in the light from the hotel next door. Leila was staring at me as though she were seeing something equally strange in my hair.

Then our heads were white all over, then our clothes, then the floor. Then the first brick fell from the ceiling and the walls cracked, and through the window the ranks were still approaching.

That last night, as we fought off sleep in the desert, I asked Bahr the real reason he had come home and why he was collecting all those stories. I remember what he said—like someone repeating an adage—"Because everything comes down."

At the time, I thought it was a metaphor.

Even as I pulled Leila through the doorway, the stairs were crumbling away behind us. We had no way out.

It came like a shadow—the memory of Bahr pointing up to the ceiling the day he'd told me about the village that lived in corners. I grabbed Leila's arm and hauled her back into the room, and we stood together by the concrete pillar next to the window, her back pressed against the wall and me facing her, encircling her body with my arms.

And I remembered the hospital, the doctor leading me down the long curving corridor to where Alya lay alone, caught between sleep and waking. I remembered sitting on the edge of the bed as Alya slowly opened and closed her eyes, then blinked rapidly several times as if to make certain I was there. I remembered her taking my hand and placing it gently on her stomach. Remembered her saying:

"I was going to call her Leila. But there's no her now, no anyone. Nothing left to hold anyone. They took everything out."

I sobbed.

She said, "I'm Leila."

She didn't let me call her Alya ever again.

Here we were now, down on the floor of the room, and the room shaking, and I still couldn't tell: Was this the sound of everything collapsing or was it just the marching feet down below? What's the word for the tramp of footsteps, Alya? *Waeed?*

I crawled over to the window, pulled myself up, and looked out. Faces were beginning to come clear in the hotel's glow, and now I understood why I'd felt that sense of familiarity. There was Amany Assayyid. There was Zeinhom. I thought I saw my mother and my father, who was—how odd—in the same white vest he'd always worn. And I was looking for Alya and me, walking together, but a hand snatched me back before I could see.

I turned to find her staring at me. She pulled me to her, and we sat together on the rippling floor. Holding me tight she said, "There's one thing I haven't lost. Not yet. Listen."

She brought her lips to my ear and sang me silence.